THE CAT JUMPS
and other stories

ELIZABETH BOWEN

THE CAT JUMPS

and other stories

JONATHAN CAPE
THIRTY BEDFORD SQUARE
LONDON

FIRST PUBLISHED 1934
FIRST PUBLISHED IN THE COLLECTED EDITION 1949
REPRINTED 1955
REPRINTED 1967

PRINTED IN GREAT BRITAIN BY
LOWE AND BRYDONE (PRINTERS) LIMITED, LONDON
ON PAPER MADE BY JOHN DICKINSON & CO. LTD
BOUND BY A. W. BAIN & CO. LTD, LONDON

CONTENTS

THE TOMMY CRANS

ERBERT'S feet, from dangling so long in the tram, had died of cold in his boots; he stamped the couple of coffins on blue-and-buff mosaic. In the Tommy Crans' cloak-room the pegs were too high — Uncle Archer cocked H.M.S. *Terrible* for him over a checked ulster. Tommy Cran — aslant meanwhile, in the doorway — was an enormous presence. 'Come on, now, come!' he exclaimed, and roared with impatience. You would have said he was also arriving at the Tommy Crans' Christmas party, of which one could not bear to miss a moment.

Now into the hall Mrs. Tommy Cran came swimming from elsewhere, dividing with curved little strokes the festive air — hyacinths and gunpowder. Her sleeves, in a thousand ruffles, fled from her elbows. She gained Uncle Archer's lapels and, bobbing, floated from this attachment. Uncle Archer, verifying the mistletoe, loudly kissed her face of delicate pink sugar. 'Ha!' yelled Tommy, drawing an unseen dagger. Herbert laughed with embarrassment.

'Only think, Nancy let off all the crackers before tea! She's quite wild, but there are more behind the piano. Ah, is this little Herbert? Herbert . . .'

'Very well, thank you,' said Herbert, and shook hands defensively. This was his first Christmas Day without any father; the news went before him. He had seen his mother off, very brave with the holly wreath, in the cemetery tram. She and father were spending Christmas afternoon together.

9

Mrs. Tommy Cran stooped to him, bright with a tear-glitter, then with a strong upward sweep, like an angel's, bore him to gaiety. '*Fancy* Nancy!' He fancied Nancy. So by now they would all be wearing the paper caps. Flinging back a white door, she raced Herbert elsewhere.

The room where they all sat seemed to be made of glass, it collected the whole daylight; the candles were still waiting. Over the garden, day still hung like a pink flag; over the trees like frozen feathers, the enchanted icy lake, the lawn. The table was in the window. As Herbert was brought in a clock struck four; the laughing heads all turned in a silence brief as a breath's intake. The great many gentlemen and the rejoicing ladies leaned apart; he and Nancy looked at each other gravely.

He saw Nancy, crowned and serious because she was a queen. Advanced by some urgent pushing, he made his way round the table and sat down beside her, podgily.

She said: 'How d'you do? Did you see our lake? It is all frozen. Did you ever see our lake before?'

'I never came here.'

'Did you see our two swans?'

She was so beautiful, rolling her ringlets, round with light, on her lacy shoulders, that he said rather shortly: 'I shouldn't have thought your lake was large enough for two swans.'

'It is, indeed,' said Nancy; 'it goes round the island. It's large enough for a boat.'

They were waiting, around the Christmas cake, for tea to be brought in. Mrs. Tommy Cran shook out the ribbons of her guitar and began to sing again. Very quietly, for a secret, he and Nancy crept to the window; she showed how the lake wound; he could guess how, in summer, her boat would go pushing among the lily leaves. She showed him their boat-house, rusty-red from a lamp inside, solid. 'We had a lamp put there for the poor cold swans.' (And the swans were asleep beside it). 'How old are you, Herbert?'

'Eight.'

'Oh, I'm nine. Do you play brigands?'

'I could,' said Herbert.

'Oh, I don't; I'd hate to. But I know some boys who do. Did you have many presents? Uncle Ponto brought me a train; it's more suitable for a boy, really. I could give it to you, perhaps.'

'How many uncles —— ?' began Herbert.

'Ten pretence and none really. I'm adopted, because mummy and daddy have no children. I think that's better fun, don't you?'

'Yes,' replied Herbert, after consideration; 'anybody could be born.'

All the time, Nancy had not ceased to look at him seriously and impersonally. They were both tired already by this afternoon of boisterous grown-up society; they would have liked to be quiet, and though she was loved by ten magic uncles and wore a pearl locket, and he was fat, with spectacles, and felt deformed a little from everybody's knowing about his father, they felt at ease in each other's company.

'Nancy, cut the cake!' exclaimed Mrs. Tommy, and they all clapped their hands for Nancy's attention. So the coloured candles were lit, the garden went dark with loneliness and was immediately curtained out. Two of the uncles put rugs on and bounded about the room like bears and lions; the other faces drew out a crimson band round the silver teapot. Mrs. Tommy could not bear to put down the guitar, so the teapot fell into the hands of a fuzzy lady with several husbands who cried 'Ah, don't, now!' and had to keep brushing gentlemen's hands from her waist. And all the others leaned on each other's shoulders and laughed with gladness because they had been asked to the Tommy Crans'; a dozen times everyone died of laughter and rose again, redder ghosts. Teacups whizzed down a chain of hands. Now Nancy, standing up very straight to cut the cake, was like a doll stitched upright into its box, apt, if you should cut the string at the back, to pitch right forward and break its delicate fingers.

'Oh dear,' she sighed, as the knife skidded over the icing. But nobody heard but Herbert. For someone, seeing her white frock over that palace of cake, proposed 'The health of the bride'. And an Uncle Joseph, tipping the tea about in his cup, stared and stared with juicy eyes. But nobody saw but Herbert.

'After tea,' she whispered, 'we'll go and stand on the lake.' And after tea they did, while the others played hide and seek. Herbert, once looking back through a window, saw uncles chasing the laughing aunts. It was not cold on the lake. Nancy said: 'I never believed in fairies — did you either?' She told him she had been given a white muff and was going to be an organist, with an organ of her own. She was going up to Belfast next month to dance for charity. She said she would not give him the train after all; she would give him something really her own, a pink glass greyhound that was an ornament.

When Uncle Archer and Herbert left to walk to the tram terminus, the party was at its brightest. They were singing 'Hark the herald' around the drawing-room piano: Nancy sat on her Uncle Joseph's knee, more than politely.

Uncle Archer did not want to go home either. 'That was a nice little girl,' he said. 'Eh?'

Herbert nodded. His uncle, glad that the little chap hadn't had, after all, such a dismal Christmas, pursued heartily: 'Kiss her?' Herbert looked quite blank. To tell the truth, this had never occurred to him.

He kissed Nancy later; his death, even, was indirectly caused by his loss of her; but their interchanges were never passionate, and he never knew her better than when they had been standing out on the lake, beyond the cheerful windows. Herbert's mother did not know Uncle Archer's merry friends: she had always loved to live quietly, and, as her need for comfort decreased, she and Herbert saw less, or at least as little as ever of Uncle Archer. So that for years Herbert was not taken again across Dublin to the house with the lake. Once he saw Nancy carry her white muff into a shop, but he stood rooted and did not run after her. Once he saw Mrs. Tommy Cran out in Stephen's Green throwing lollipops to the ducks: but he did not approach; there was nothing to say. He was sent to school, where he painfully learnt to be natural with boys: his sight got no better; they said he must wear glasses all his life. Years later, however, when Herbert was thirteen, the Crans gave a dancing-party and did not forget him. He danced once with Nancy; she was silenter now, but she said: 'Why did you never come back again?' He could not explain; he trod on her toes and danced heavily on. A Chinese lantern blazed up, and in the confusion he lost her. That evening he saw Mrs. Tommy in tears in the conservatory. Nancy clung, pressing her head, with its drooping pink ribbons, to Mrs. Cran's shoulder; pressing, perhaps, the shoulder against the head. Soon it was all right again and Mrs. Tommy led off in 'Sir Roger', but Nancy was like a ghost who presently vanished. A week afterwards he had a letter:

Please meet me to tea at Mitchell's; I want your advice specially.

She was distracted: she had come in to Dublin to sell her gold wrist-watch. The Tommy Crans had lost all their money — it wasn't fair to expect them to keep it; they were generous and gay. Nancy had to think hard what must they all do. Herbert went round with her from jeweller to jeweller: these all laughed and paid her nothing but compliments. Her face, with those delicate lovely eyebrows, grew tragic under the fur cap; it rained continuously; she and Herbert looked with incredulity into the grown-up faces: they wondered how one could penetrate far into life without despair. At last a man on the quays gave her eight-and-six for the watch. Herbert, meanwhile, had spent eight shillings of his pocket-money on their cab — and, even so, her darling feet were sodden. They were surprised to see, from the window, Tommy Cran jump from an outside car and run joyfully into the Shelbourne. It turned out he had raised some more money from somewhere — as he deserved.

So he sold the house with the lake and moved to an ornamental castle by Dublin Bay. In spite of the grey scene, the transitory light from the sea, the terrace here was gay with urns of geraniums, magnificent with a descent of steps — scrolls and whorls of balustrade, all the grandeur of stucco. Here the band played for their afternoon parties, and here, when they were twenty and twenty-one, Herbert asked Nancy to marry him.

A pug harnessed with bells ran jingling about the terrace. 'Oh, I don't know, Herbert; I don't know.'

'Do you think you don't love me?'

'I don't know whom I love. Everything would have to be different. Herbert, I don't see how we are ever to live; we seem to know everything. Surely there should be something for us we don't know?' She shut her eyes; they kissed seriously and searchingly. In his arms her body felt soft and voluminous; he could not touch her because of a great fur coat. The coat had been a surprise from Tommy Cran, who loved to give presents on delightful occasions — for now they were off to the Riviera. They were sailing in four days; Nancy and Mrs. Tommy had still all their shopping to do, all his money to spend — he loved them both to be elegant. There was that last party to give before leaving home. Mrs. Tommy could hardly leave the telephone; crossing London, they were to give yet another party, at the Euston Hotel.

'And how could I leave them?' she asked. 'They're my business.'

'Because they are not quite your parents?'

'Oh, no,' she said, eyes reproachful for the misunderstanding he had put up, she knew, only from bitterness. 'They would be my affair whoever I was. Don't you see, they're like that.'

The Tommy Crans returned from the Riviera subdued, and gave no more parties than they could avoid. They hung sun-yellow curtains, in imitation of the Midi, in all the castle windows, and fortified themselves against despair. They warned their friends they were ruined; they honestly were — and there were heartfelt evenings of consolation. After such evenings Mrs. Tommy, awaking heavily, whimpered in Nancy's arms, and Tommy approached silence. They had the highest opinion of Nancy, and were restored by her confidence. She knew they would be all right; she assured them they were the best, the happiest people: they were popular — look how Life came back again and again to beg their pardon. And, just to show them, she accepted Jeremy Neath and his thousands. So the world could see she was lucky; the world saw the Tommy Crans and their daughter had all the luck. To Herbert she explained nothing. She expected everything of him, on behalf of the Tommy Crans.

The two Crans were distracted by her apotheosis from the

incident of their ruin. They had seen her queen of a perpetual Christmas party for six months before they themselves came down magnificently, like an empire. Then Nancy came to fetch them over to England, where her husband had found a small appointment for Tommy, excuse for a pension. But Tommy would not want that long; he had a scheme already, a stunner, a certainty; you just wrote to a hundred people and put in half a crown. That last night he ran about with the leaflets, up and down the uncarpeted castle stairs that were his no longer. He offered to let Herbert in on it; he would yet see Herbert a rich man.

Herbert and Nancy walked after dark on the terrace: she looked ill, tired; she was going to have a baby.

'When I asked you to marry me,' he said, 'you never answered. You've never answered yet.'

She said: 'There was no answer. We could never have loved each other and we shall always love each other. We are related.'

Herbert, a heavy un-young young man, walked, past desperation, beside her. He did not want peace, but a sword. He returned again and again to the unique moment of her strangeness to him before, as a child, she had spoken. Before, bewildered by all the laughter, he had realized she also was silent.

'You never played games,' he said, 'or believed in fairies, or anything. I'd have played any game your way; I'd have been good at them. You let them pull all the crackers before tea: now I'd have loved those crackers. That day we met at Mitchell's to sell your watch, you wouldn't have sugar cakes, though I wanted to comfort you. You never asked me out to go round the island in your boat; I'd have died to do that. I never even saw your swans awake. You hold back everything from me and expect me to understand. Why should I understand: In the name of God, what game are we playing?'

'But you do understand?'

'Oh, God,' he cried in revulsion. 'I don't want to! And now you're going to have a stranger child.'

Her sad voice in the dark said: 'You said then, "Anybody could be born!" Herbert, you and I have nothing to do with children — this must be a child like them.'

As they turned back to face the window, her smile and voice were tender, but not for him. In the brightly lit stripped room the Tommy Crans walked about together, like lovers in their freedom from one another. They talked of the fortune to be made, the child to be born. Tommy flung his chest out and moved his arms freely in air he did not possess; here and there, pink leaflets fluttered into the dark. The Tommy Crans would go on for ever and be continued; their seed should never fail.

THE GOOD GIRL

'. . . AND restored my faith in life,' concluded Captain
Monteparnesi. He straightened out his gloves to
the last finger, laid them down on the table, and
gazed at Monica.

She could only gaze at the Alps. It was solemn, wonderfully
like church. She was twenty-two: this, her third proposal,
seemed a distinct echo. The Alps, so distantly, brightly
painted over the bright lake, offered no inspiration, though
from this very terrace they must often have been consulted.
His passion, however, was of the purest; he was a Milanese
of good family . . . He was still waiting; she did not know
what to say.

The evening of her arrival, in April half-light, they had
discovered themselves advancing towards each other down an
immense corridor. They trod a magenta carpet fresh as the
spring season; to this, in passing, he had lowered his eyes
delicately. They passed: for both the perspective became
forlorn. Those were seconds charged with fatality. At dinner,
he, from his distant table, gave their party his courteously
veiled attention. Naturally it had been Dagmar who, ash-
blonde, made play with her dark eyelids. Yet Monica had
what her French friend, the Baronne de Besserat, called a
'je ne sais quoi'. That night, this had been in evidence, had
been remarkable even to Uncle Porgie — and heaven knew
he was preoccupied! Uncle Porgie, lifting his glass to twinkle
in the pink lamplight, paid Monica tribute: 'She's a dam'

pretty girl, and a good girl, too!' Yet, all the time, under the table, he had been pursuing Dagmar's foot. When hers withdrew, his gave chase with audible pounces over the parquet: the pursuit gained in speed and compass, until there seemed to be no place under their table for the feet of a good girl.

Uncle Porgie was not anyone's uncle. That was his disappointment, he said; he had no niece. He had invited Monica to call him uncle also, since she was Dagmar's cousin, and when he invited her to accompany them to Italy, Dagmar declared she must. So Monica gently bounced across Italy in the back seat of the Rolls, beside the valet. . . .

Captain Monteparnesi now tenderly coughed.

'Life,' replied Monica, 'is so difficult.'

'I place my life in your hands,' he said helpfully.

'Oh, thank you . . . Thank you, Captain Monteparnesi.'

So she got up carefully, as though balancing his life. She needed time to think – he understood perfectly. He kissed her right, then her left hand, then returned both regretfully. She walked away between the attendant tulips.

Captain Monteparnesi brought out his pocket-book from against his heart and made some calculations. He sighed; he was not a rich man. Then he went round to the garage for another look at the Rolls-Royce.

The Angelus came sweetly across the lake, but Dagmar, sitting out on her loggia, frowned at a tulip-tree in extravagant blossom. She was beautiful (arms, neck, of supple ivory; her pale hair, brushed, you would think, with a gold-powdered brush, petal-curled at the nape), but that does not keep a girl going for ever. And nothing could have been more provoking than Uncle Porgie, who was kissing his way up her arm.

'Mind,' she said, and pushed at his head crossly as Monica

stepped through the window. Their gold wicker chairs creaked.

'Darlin', where *have* you been? I've been so lonely. We've been talking about Rome.'

Uncle Porgie, straightening his tie, smiled at Monica in the friendliest way possible. Might not Rome be jolly? He knew of a thundering good hotel.

'But it's so far,' said Monica, and had, with surprise, a small pang. The heart, then, was not intact.

'No, no; surely it's all in Italy?'

The Rolls-Royce did, it is true, make short work of Italy, which is a country smaller than you would think. The Rolls had eaten up the Milan-Varese *auto strada* at what Uncle Porgie called a smooth eighty. He had often heard of this *auto strada*, on which there is no speed limit, and now he only regretted that the antiquities of this remarkable country could not be ranged for inspection along its smooth white kerbs. At Varese the *auto strada* had come to an end unaccountably, so here they all were; it seemed nice. You sat on the terrace, where tulips lifted gay little cups of light. In immediate response to the suggestion, electric bells depending from plane-trees connected the terrace with the bar. Judas- and almond-trees frivolled among the austere cedars; cypresses marched to the lake from terrace to terrace, and wax-yellow friesias sweetened the April twilight. Placards forbidding children to play on the terrace discouraged Italian family life; English and Americans, fervently elsewhere, overlooked Varese. Antiquities did not impend; the view, though tasteful, was unexigent. The inhabitants of Varese were occupied in the manufacture of stockings; it seemed delightful that they should be so busy. Work, Uncle Porgie believed, kept men happy — that and the society of beautiful women. He sighed often, looking at the lake; he was a bit of an idealist. Visitors, arriving in pairs down the *auto strada* in a succession of whirring flashes, were expected to provide their own entertainment; in prolonged seclusion they fulfilled the expectations of the management. Cherry-clad little boys shot up in the lifts with bottles of champagne in buckets.

All this seemed strange to Monica. She had finished reading her book about Leonardo da Vinci, then, the afternoon after her arrival, had taken a walking-stick and the hotel dog and walked by high-walled alleys down to the lake. Here she found mud-flats, washing, stark damp reeds, no one about. The lake was intended for distant scenery. She spoke Italian to a child who ran away, then she walked up again. On the terrace she had come upon Captain Monteparnesi, engaged in sadness. He patted the dog. 'I love dogs,' he said, 'it is almost a madness with me.' In the course of their conversation he had forthwith explained: he was a solitary man, a widower. It was fortunate that he loved nature. 'But in the heart,' he said, 'of so much beauty, one feels oneself alone.'

In fact, he spoke English remarkably well. Sport, he had said, was also a madness with him. It was to be seen that Monica was a sports-girl. That was on Monday. Since, it had all blossomed . . . Today, Thursday, they talked of going away to Rome.

'I'm sorry you don't like Rome,' Dagmar said, discouraged. 'It sounds to me so historic. Uncle Porgie, if you are going down to the bar, let Alessandro know that I'd like a side-car. He'll send it up.'

Uncle Porgie, blowing out his cheeks (like a *putto* attending Aurora in one of those rather confused processions), patted Dagmar's knee, then trotted down to the bar. He was most suggestible.

'*Mmwaow*,' yawned Dagmar. She threw her arms over her head, and kicked one of her gilt-heeled slippers across the loggia.

Monica blushed with honesty. 'Dagmar . . . I do think we ought to be clear, you know, about Uncle Porgie. I had no idea when we left England that he was so much . . . *not* an uncle as all that.'

'Oh, dear,' Dagmar said, resigned. 'I am so stupid. I never know what anybody is talking about.'

'I do sometimes wonder if we ought not to go home.'

'Oh, I'm not going back by train; I can tell you that definitely. Darlin', you wouldn't be mean and leave me? After all, Monica, men aren't everything; I've never allowed them to count in my life.'

She should know. Men had not been nice to her. She had had to break off several engagements and leave a husband. Uncle Porgie called her his brave little woman . . . 'Darlin', let Alessandro in; he's got my side-car.' Alessandro was knocking portentously, like a postman — the hotel service was most discreet.

Monica put out Dagmar's evening things for her, untangled the long pearl rope, and opened some new powder. It made Dagmar tired to watch her; she sighed and went through to the bath. Soon she said plaintively, through the open door, 'Talk to me; tell me things. I get so bored, all alone here in my bath.' Steam, curling through the ivory bedroom, clouded the mirrors; Monica, relieved of her own pink reflection, was able to bring out: 'As a matter of fact, Captain Monteparnesi wants me to marry him.'

'Wants you to what?'

'Marry him.'

'Who does?'

'Captain Monteparnesi.'

23

'Oh, him.' There were some seconds of splashing and slow reflection. 'It's a pity his legs are like that.'

'He was a cavalry officer.'

'He must have held on to the horse very tight with his legs. Even so, they are short.'

'I do like him best sitting down. But he seems very idealistic and fond of the open air.'

'Italians are fearfully passionate,' said Dagmar gloomily. 'I know a girl who got bitten by an Italian. But, as I said, that is just their way. Does he make love in English?'

(Dagmar did not quite understand.) Monica said: 'He tells me about his life.'

'Oh, that kind! Monica, come and wrap little Dagmar up in a big bath towel. Really, I don't know what you will do in Rome with all those Italians. I think you're marvellous. Look, you must introduce him to us after dinner; after all, I am your chaperon, and Uncle Porgie is practically your guardian. I really think, Monica, you should have done that before, when you felt all this coming on.'

'But I can never find you.'

'Oh, nonsense, darlin'; we are always about.'

The introduction was not a success. Uncle Porgie could not, somehow, stomach a dago, but did his best. Monica, in pale pink, found herself sitting closer to Captain Monteparnesi than she had expected. Captain Monteparnesi attentively looked at Dagmar, who wore her air of floating lily-wise on the social current. Her smiles went hesitatingly to all of them, tender as young butterflies; sometimes her smiles for Captain Monteparnesi were frequent and flashing.

They sat grouped by an indoor fountain. 'They are nervous,' said Captain Monteparnesi, pointing to the goldfish. 'Goldfish are highly nervous, impossible to tame.'

'I hear you are fond of animals?'

24

'I had a horse once that was shot under me.'

'Oh, dear, whatever did you do then?'

But something swelled in Monica's throat at the thought of the horse; she wanted to drop her head and weep where there had been an epaulette.

'Horses,' said Uncle Porgie, 'are like women, temperamental, fickle. Never know where you have 'em.' And — oh, horror! — his foot went creeping towards Dagmar's.

'It would make any goldfish nervous,' exclaimed Monica quickly, 'living under a fountain.'

Her friend replied, 'One accustoms oneself to everything.' He behaved, in fact, with infinite sensibility. But afterwards, out on the terrace, he confessed he did not care for her aunt's lover; he did not find him an English type. 'But you,' he added, 'are my flower.'

She had not the heart to disagree with him. 'Pure!' he exclaimed, and kissed her shoulder. Behind them, the band thrilled in the empty ballroom. Tulips, gold ghosts, crowded up to the windows; cypresses gathered unseen, tense. She felt quite his own. But she also felt bound to explain: 'She is not my aunt, and he is her uncle.' He exclaimed: 'My flower!' (ravished by her remark), kissing her as low on the chest as her *decolletage* permitted. 'Oh, I don't think——' But, murmuring indistinctly, he had begun to be rather Italian. She had never produced this effect before. '*Tiens!*' she could have exclaimed. Because really—— But then she thought of her mother at Chislehurst, and of her old school, of which she hoped never to be unworthy. And from the night air, or because heaven had intervened, she sneezed, loudly and uncontrollably.

Stepping back from the portico as she went in, he accepted her good night. He blew his nose; you would think he had never panted with great emotion; it became once more evident that his passion was of the purest. How much relieved she was.

But the lounge was staring and still; a great many mirrors reflected its emptiness. Everybody was elsewhere; no one else in the hotel tried to be good. The lift sighed up with Monica. Dagmar's room was empty; an outraged little clock ticked angrily in the darkness; below, the band still throbbed on. The band had been hours silent before Dagmar came up.

In the course of the next day Monica found herself becoming by imperceptible degrees engaged to Captain Monteparnesi. He constituted public opinion, for she saw no one else. Dagmar and Uncle Porgie were busy always; round corners she heard chairs creak as they bent over maps of Rome. That night she received, with surprise but gratification, what appeared to be the betrothal kiss; he left a rose in her place at dinner; afterwards they danced a waltz, a foxtrot and then a one-step together in the empty ballroom. The lonely band appeared very much encouraged. Couples looked languidly in at the windows, then went away. Then he had a bottle of champagne brought out to the terrace; they drank and, feeling very much moved by the solemnity of the occasion, she talked to him of her mother, then he spoke of his mother.

Then a terrible thing happened. They had walked down the terraces, and, among the lemons and cypresses, had a conversation about infinity, touching also upon ideals. The conversation, with some caresses in character with its subject, naturally prolonged itself. When they returned the hotel was shut up; not a light shining; a clock behind in the town did indeed strike two. In this leafy lakeside retreat one retired early; their behaviour had been without precedent. Such a thing as this had never happened to Monica; she reproached her Guglielmo with some sharpness. She leaned on the door and sniffed with so much despair that he was provoked to ask her point-blank if she were really an heiress. She sobbed *indeed* not; he comforted her politely. He said, 'You have always your charm.' It was a long time before anybody came. Then the night-porter was horrified.

Dagmar was worse than horrified. She was surprised. She pointed out, this was not what one had expected. Next morning, curled up in bed, curtains drawn across the insistent daylight, she said it seemed obvious they must now go at once to Rome. She doubted if the hotel would keep them, now this had happened. The night-porter had told the waiters, the waiters had told all the chambermaids; she said Uncle Porgie was really very much shocked. He was particular who Dagmar went about with; he had always said she could not be too careful. Till now, he had thought of Monica as a nice friend.

'Well, really . . .' said Monica.

'I tell you how it will be, Monica; you will end by having a baby. A girl cannot be too careful.'

'Well, really . . .'

'And an Italian and everything.'

'Whatever . . .'

'Darlin', Dagmar's being very, very loyal——'

Trembling with indignation, Monica sped down to the terrace, for Guglielmo. But, courteously, he inclined to her through a crowd: this way, that way — right and left of a lady's head. The terrace was dark with Italian ladies who sat about him.

This morning, as a surprise, his relatives had all come out by train from Milan: his aunt, his mother, his widowed sister with her children, his sister who had still to marry and wore a dark moustache. He was pleased; he had missed them; he was accustomed to family life. They sat in black, with black furs, in the ardent sunshine, complimenting him upon the lake, while the Alps appeared to draw nearer in fascination. They sipped *aranciata*, but did not remove their gloves. In so large a family, necessarily, there has always been a bereavement.

Dagmar, looking down from her loggia, knew that her cousin could not have sinned with a man with so large and black a family, And once more it seemed unlikely to her that Monica ever would sin (in recognition of this, passing later through Milan, she made Uncle Porgie buy Monica a pair of coral drop ear-rings: for some people life held nothing). For Monica it was simpler; as he stood up to bow she really noticed his legs for the first time: she had never loved him. Naturally, however, she was still very much upset. She snipped the head off a tulip and walked away; it was her only gesture.

His family, evidently, were great with some information; they exchanged glances, and soon it transpired they brought good news. His unmarried cousin Liliana, who had so tenderly asked for him since their childhood, had become, last Friday, through the suicide of an uncle, direct heiress to the Piselli millions; so it became his duty to leave the divine panorama and hurry back to Milan. Young men might already be on her doorstep. Now his cousin Liliana, though no sports-girl, did not keep him up past midnight discussing infinity. He was seriously tired this morning, and had a slight chill on the liver. Not without emotion, he shortly afterwards wrote his farewell to Monica. 'You restored my faith in life,' he wrote; 'you could not have done more. But there are sterner calls.' Meanwhile his mother, a woman of tact, quietly packed for him. Then the family left the hotel together, quickly and quietly. It was not till months afterwards that she heard how nearly he had been entangled with an English girl of doubtful reputation.

Twenty minutes later the Rolls-Royce, bonnet turned towards Rome, passed the little party on its way to the station. Dagmar remarked: 'How is it that good Italian women are always dusty?' Uncle Porgie had no idea. Monica, eyes shut, hoped this might be the last she would hear of virtue.

But she was not to be so fortunate.

THE CAT JUMPS

A FTER the Bentley murder, Rose Hill stood empty two years. Lawns mounted to meadows; white paint peeled from the balconies; the sun, looking more constantly, less fearfully in than sightseer's eyes through the naked windows, bleached the floral wallpapers. The week after the execution Harold Bentley's legatees had placed the house on the books of the principal agents, London and local. But though sunny, up to date, and convenient, though so delightfully situated over the Thames valley (above flood level), within easy reach of a golfcourse, Rose Hill, while frequently viewed, remained unpurchased. Dreadful associations apart, the privacy of the place had been violated; with its terraced garden, lily-pond and pergola cheerfully rose-encrusted, the public had been made too familiar. On the domestic scene too many eyes had burnt the impress of their horror. Moreover, that pearly bathroom, that bedroom with wide outlook over a loop of the Thames ... '*The Rose Hill Horror*': headlines flashed up at the very sound of the name. 'Oh, *no*, dear!' many wives had exclaimed, drawing their husbands hurriedly from the gate. 'Come away!' they had urged crumpling the agent's order to view as though the house were advancing upon them. And husbands came away — with a backward glance at the garage. Funny to think a chap who was hanged had kept his car there.

The Harold Wrights, however, were not deterred. They had light, bright, shadowless, thoroughly disinfected minds.

They believed that they disbelieved in most things but were unprejudiced; they enjoyed frank discussions. They dreaded nothing but inhibitions: they had no inhibitions. They were pious agnostics, earnest for social reform; they explained everything to their children, and were annoyed to find their children could not sleep at nights because they thought there was a complex under the bed. They knew all crime to be pathological, and read their murders only in scientific books. They had vita glass put into all their windows. No family, in fact, could have been more unlike the mistaken Harold Bentleys.

Rose Hill, from the first glance, suited the Wrights admirably. They were in search of a cheerful week-end house with a nice atmosphere, where their friends could join them for frank discussions, and their own and their friends' children 'run wild' during the summer months. Harold Wright, who had a good head, got the agent to knock six hundred off the quoted price of the house. 'That unfortunate affair,' he murmured. Jocelyn commended his inspiration. Otherwise, they did not give the Bentleys another thought.

The Wrights had the floral wallpapers all stripped off and the walls cream-washed; they removed some disagreeably thick pink shades from the electricity and had the paint renewed inside and out. (The front of the house was bracketed over with balconies, like an overmantel.) Their bedroom mantelpiece, stained by the late Mrs. Bentley's cosmetics, had to be scrubbed with chemicals. Also, they had removed from the rock-garden Mrs. Bentley's little dog's memorial tablet, with a quotation on it from *Indian Love Lyrics*. Jocelyn Wright, looking into the unfortunate bath — *the* bath, so square and opulent, with its surround of nacreous tiles — said, laughing lightly, she supposed anyone *else* would have had that bath changed. 'Not that that would be possible,' she added; 'the bath's built in . . . I've always wanted a built-in bath.'

Harold and Jocelyn turned from the bath to look down at the cheerful river shimmering under a spring haze. All the way down the slope cherry-trees were in blossom. Life should be simplified for the Wrights; they were fortunate in their mentality.

After an experimental week-end, without guests or children, only one thing troubled them: a resolute stuffiness, upstairs and down — due presumably, to the house's having been so long shut up — a smell of unsavoury habitation, of rich cigarette-smoke stale in the folds of unaired curtains, of scent spilled on unbrushed carpets, an alcoholic smell — persistent in their perhaps too sensitive nostrils after days of airing, doors and windows open, in rooms drenched thoroughly with sun and wind. They told each other it came from the parquet; they didn't like it, somehow. They had the parquet taken up — at great expense — and put down plain oak floors.

In their practical way, the Wrights now set out to expel, live out, live down, almost (had the word had place in their vocabulary) to 'lay' the Bentleys. Deferred by trouble over the parquet, their occupation of Rose Hill, which should have dated from mid-April, did not begin till the end of May. Throughout a week, Jocelyn had motored from town daily, so that the final installation of themselves and the children was able to coincide with their first week-end party — they asked down five of their friends to warm the house.

That first Friday, everything was auspicious; afternoon sky blue as the garden irises; later, a full moon pendent over the river; a night so warm that, after midnight, their enlightened friends, in pyjamas, could run on the blanched lawns in a state of high though rational excitement. Jane, Jacob and Janet, their admirably spaced-out children, kept awake by the moonlight, hailed their elders out of the nursery skylight. Jocelyn waved to them: they never had been repressed.

The girl Muriel Barker was found looking up the terraces at the house a shade doubtfully. 'You know,' she said, 'I do rather wonder they don't feel . . . *sometimes* . . . you know what I mean?'

'No,' replied her companion, a young scientist.

Muriel sighed. 'No one would mind if it had been just a short sharp shooting. But it was so . . . prolonged. It went on all over the house. Do you remember?' she said timidly.

'No,' replied Mr. Cartaret. 'It didn't interest me.'

'Oh, nor me either!' agreed Muriel quickly, but added: 'How he must have hated her. . . .'

The scientist, sleepy, yawned frankly and referred her to Krafft Ebing. But Muriel went to bed with *Alice in Wonderland*; she went to sleep with the lights on. She was not, as Jocelyn realized later, the sort of girl to have asked at all.

Next morning was overcast; in the afternoon it rained, suddenly and heavily — interrupting, for some, tennis, for others, a pleasant discussion, in a punt, on marriage under the Soviet. Defeated, they all rushed in. Jocelyn went round from room to room, shutting tightly the rain-lashed casements along the front of the house. These continued to rattle; the balconies creaked. An early dusk set in; an oppressive, almost visible moisture, up from the darkening river, pressed on the panes like a presence and slid through the house. The party gathered in the library, round an expansive but thinly burning fire. Harold circulated photographs of modern architecture; they discussed these tendencies. Then Mrs. Monkhouse, sniffing, exclaimed: 'Who uses "Trèfle Incarnat"?'

'Now, *who* ever would——' her hostess began scornfully. Then from the hall came a howl, scuffle, a thin shriek. They sat too still; in the dusky library Mr. Cartaret laughed out loud.

Harold Wright, indignantly throwing open the door, revealed Jane and Jacob rolling at the foot of the stairs, biting each other, their faces dark with uninhibited passion. Bumping alternate heads against the foot of the banisters, they shrieked in concert.

'Extraordinary,' said Harold; 'they've never done that before. They have always understood each other so well.'

'I wouldn't do that,' advised Jocelyn, raising her voice slightly; 'you'll hurt your teeth. Other teeth won't grow at once, you know.'

'You should let them find that out for themselves,' disapproved Edward Cartaret, taking up the *New Statesman*. Harold, in perplexity, shut the door on his children, who soon stunned each other to silence.

Meanwhile, Sara and Talbot Monkhouse, Muriel Barker and Theodora Smith, had drawn together over the fire in a tight little knot. Their voices twanged with excitement. By that shock, just now, something seemed to have been released. Even Cartaret gave them half his attention. They were discussing *crime passionnel*.

'Of course, if that's what they really *want* to discuss . . .' thought Jocelyn. But it did seem unfortunate. Partly from an innocent desire to annoy her visitors, partly because the room felt awful — you would have thought fifty people had been there for a week — she went across and opened one of the windows, admitting a pounce of damp wind. They all turned, startled, to hear rain crash on the lead of an upstairs balcony. Muriel's voice was left in forlorn solo: 'Dragged herself . . . whining "Harold" . . .'

Harold Wright looked remarkably conscious. Jocelyn said brightly, 'Whatever *are* you talking about?' But, unfortunately, Harold, on almost the same breath, suggested: 'Let's leave that family alone, shall we?' Their friends all felt they might

35

not be asked again. Though they did feel, plaintively, that they had been being natural. However, they disowned Muriel, who, getting up abruptly, said she thought she'd like to go for a walk in the rain before dinner. Nobody accompanied her.

Later, overtaking Mrs. Monkhouse on the stairs, Muriel confided: absolutely, she could not stand Edward Cartaret. She could hardly bear to be in the room with him. He seemed so ... cruel. Cold-blooded? No, she meant cruel. Sara Monkhouse, going into Jocelyn's room for a chat (at her entrance Jocelyn started violently), told Jocelyn that Muriel could not stand Edward, could hardly bear to be in a room with him. 'Pity,' said Jocelyn. 'I had thought they might do for each other.' Jocelyn and Sara agreed that Muriel was unrealized: what she ought to have was a baby. But when Sara, dressing, told Talbot Monkhouse that Muriel could not stand Edward, and Talbot said Muriel was unrealized, Sara was furious. The Monkhouses, who never did quarrel, quarrelled bitterly, and were late for dinner. They would have been later if the meal itself had not been delayed by an outburst of sex-antagonism between the nice Jacksons, a couple imported from London to run the house. Mrs. Jackson, putting everything in the oven, had locked herself into her room.

'Curious,' said Harold; 'the Jacksons' relations to each other always seemed so modern. They have the most intelligent discussions.'

Theodora said she had been re-reading Shakespeare — this brought them point-blank up against *Othello*. Harold, with Titanic force, wrenched round the conversation to relativity: about this no one seemed to have anything to say but Edward Cartaret. And Muriel, who by some mischance had again been placed beside him, sat deathly, turning down her dark-rimmed eyes. In fact, on the intelligent sharp-featured faces all round the table something — perhaps simply a clearness — seemed to be lacking, as though these were wax faces for one fatal instant exposed to a furnace. Voices came out from some dark interiority; in each conversational interchange a mutual vote of no confidence was implicit. You would have said that each personality had been attacked by some kind of decomposition.

'No moon tonight,' complained Sara Monkhouse. Never mind, they would have a cosy evening; they would play paper games, Jocelyn promised.

'If you can see,' said Harold. 'Something seems to be going wrong with the light.'

Did Harold think so? They had all noticed the light seemed to be losing quality, as though a film, smoke-like, were creeping over the bulbs. The light, thinning, darkening, seemed to contract round each lamp into a blurred aura. They had noticed, but, each with a proper dread of his own subjectivity, had not spoken.

'Funny stuff, electricity,' Harold said.

Mr. Cartaret could not agree with him.

Though it was late, though they yawned and would not play paper games, they were reluctant to go to bed. You would have supposed a delightful evening. Jocelyn was not gratified.

The library stools, rugs and divans were strewn with Krafft Ebing, Freud, Forel, Weiniger and the heterosexual volume of Havelock Ellis. (Harold had thought it right to install his reference library; his friends hated to discuss without basis.) The volumes were pressed open with paper-knives and small pieces of modern statuary; stooping from one to another, purposeful as a bee, Edward Cartaret read extracts aloud to Harold, to Talbot Monkhouse, and to Theodora Smith, who stitched *gros point* with resolution. At the far end of the library under a sallow drip from a group of electric candles, Mrs. Monkhouse and Miss Barker shared an ottoman, spines pressed rigid against the wall. Tensely one spoke, one listened.

'And these,' thought Jocelyn, leaning back with her eyes shut between the two groups, 'are the friends I liked to have in my life. Pellucid, sane. . . .'

It was remarkable how much Muriel knew. Sara, very much shocked, edged up till their thighs touched. You would have thought the Harold Bentleys had been Muriel's relatives. Surely, Sara attempted, in one's large, bright world one did not think of these things? Practically, they did not exist! Surely Muriel should not . . . But Muriel looked at her strangely.

'Did you know,' she said, 'that one of Mrs. Bentley's hands was found in the library?'

Sara, smiling a little awkwardly, licked her lip. 'Oh,' she said.

'But the fingers were in the dining-room. He began there.'

'Why isn't he in Broadmoor?'

'That defence failed. He didn't really subscribe to it. He said having done what he wanted was worth anything.'

'Oh!'

'Yes, he was nearly lynched . . . She dragged herself upstairs. She couldn't lock any doors — naturally. One maid — her maid — got shut into the house with them: he'd sent all the others away. For a long time everything seemed so quiet: the maid crept out and saw Harold Bentley sitting half-way upstairs, finishing a cigarette. All the lights were full on. He nodded to her and dropped the cigarette through the banisters. Then she saw the . . . the state of the hall. He went upstairs after Mrs. Bentley, saying: 'Lucinda!' He looked into room after room, whistling; then he said '*Here we are,*' and shut a door after him.

'The maid fainted. When she came to, it was still going on, upstairs . . . Harold Bentley had locked all the garden doors; there were locks even on the French windows. The maid couldn't get out. Everything she touched was . . . sticky. At last she broke a pane and got through. As she ran down the garden — the lights were on all over the house — she saw Harold Bentley moving about in the bathroom. She fell right over the edge of a terrace and one of the tradesmen picked her up next day.

'Doesn't it seem odd, Sara, to think of Jocelyn in that bath?'

Finishing her recital, Muriel turned on Sara an ecstatic and brooding look that made her almost beautiful. Sara fumbled with a cigarette; match after match failed her. 'Muriel, *you* ought to see a specialist.'

Muriel held out her hand for a cigarette. 'He put her heart in her hat-box. He said it belonged in there.'

'You had no right to come here. It was most unfair on Jocelyn. Most . . . indelicate.'

Muriel, to whom the word was, properly, unfamiliar, eyed incredulously Sara's lips.

'How dared you come?'

'I thought I might like it. I thought I ought to fulfil myself. I'd never had any experience of these things.'

'*Muriel* . . .'

'Besides, I wanted to meet Edward Cartaret. Several people said we were made for each other. Now, of course, I shall never marry. Look what comes of it . . . I must say, Sara, I wouldn't be you or Jocelyn. Shut up all night with a man all alone — I don't know how you dare sleep. I've arranged to sleep with Theodora, and we shall barricade the door. I noticed something about Edward Cartaret the moment I arrived: a kind of insane glitter. He is utterly pathological. He's got instruments in his room, in that black bag. Yes, I looked. Did you notice the way he went on and on about cutting up that cat, and the way Talbot and Harold listened?'

Sara, looking furtively round the room, saw Mr. Cartaret making passes over the head of Theodora Smith with a paper-knife. Both appeared to laugh heartily, but in silence.

'Here we are,' said Harold, showing his teeth, smiling.

He stood over Muriel with a siphon in one hand, glass in the other.

At this point Jocelyn, rising, said she, for one, intended to go to bed.

Jocelyn's bedroom curtains swelled a little over the noisy window. The room was stuffy and — insupportable, so that she did not know where to turn. The house, fingered outwardly by the wind that dragged unceasingly past the walls, was, within, a solid silence: silence heavy as flesh. Jocelyn dropped her wrap to the floor, then watched how its feathered edges crept a little. A draught came in, under her bathroom door.

Jocelyn turned away in despair and hostility from the strained, pale woman looking at her from her oblong glass. She said aloud, 'There *is* no fear'; then, within herself, heard this taken up: 'But the death fear, that one is not there to relate! If the spirit, dismembered in agony, dies before the body! If the spirit, in the whole knowledge of its dissolution, drags from chamber to chamber, drops from plane to plane of awareness (as from knife to knife down an oubliette), shedding, receiving agony! Till, long afterwards, death, with its little pain, is established in the indifferent body.' There was no comfort: death (now at every turn and instant claiming her) was, in its every possible manifestation, violent death: ultimately, she was to be given up to terror.

Undressing, shocked by the iteration of her reflected movements, she flung a towel over the glass. With what desperate eyes of appeal, at Sara's door, she and Sara had looked at each other, clung with their looks — and parted. She could have sworn she heard Sara's bolt slide softly to. But what then, subsequently, of Talbot? And what — she eyed her own bolt, so bright (and, for the late Mrs. Bentley, so ineffective) — what of Harold?

'It's atavistic!' she said aloud, in the dark-lit room, and, kicking her slippers away, got into bed. She took *Erewhon* from the rack, but lay rigid, listening. As though snatched by a movement, the towel slipped from the mirror beyond her bed-end. She faced the two eyes of an animal in extremity, eyes black, mindless. The clock struck two: she had been waiting an hour.

On the floor, her feathered wrap shivered again all over. She heard the other door of the bathroom very stealthily open, then shut. Harold moved in softly, heavily, knocked against the side of the bath, and stood still. He was quietly whistling.

'Why didn't I understand? He must always have hated me. It's tonight he's been waiting for . . . *He wanted this house.* His look, as we went upstairs. . . .'

She shrieked: 'Harold!'

Harold, so softly whistling, remained behind the imperturbable door, remained quite still . . . 'He's *listening* for me . . .' One pin-point of hope at the tunnel-end: to get to Sara, to Theodora, to Muriel. Unmasked, incautious, with a long tearing sound of displaced air, Jocelyn leapt from the bed to the door.

But her door had been locked from the outside.

With a strange rueful smile, like an actress, Jocelyn, skirting the foot of the two beds, approached the door of the bathroom. 'At least I have still . . . my feet.' For for some time the heavy body of Mrs. Bentley, tenacious of life, had been dragging itself from room to room. '*Harold!*' she said to the silence, face close to the door.

The door opened on Harold, looking more dreadfully at her than she had imagined. With a quick, vague movement he roused himself from his meditation. Therein he had assumed the entire burden of Harold Bentley. Forces he did not know of assembling darkly, he had faced for untold ages the imperturbable door to his wife's room. She would be there, densely, smotheringly there. She lay like a great cat, always, over the mouth of his life.

The Harolds, superimposed on each other, stood searching the bedroom strangely. Taking a step forward, shutting the door behind him:

'Here we are,' said Harold.

Jocelyn went down heavily. Harold watched.

Harold Wright was appalled. Jocelyn had fainted: Jocelyn never had fainted before. He shook, he fanned, he applied restoratives. His perplexed thoughts fled to Sara — oh, Sara certainly. 'Hi!' he cried, 'Sara!' and successively fled from each to each of the locked doors. There was no way out.

Across the passage a door throbbed to the maniac drumming of Sara Monkhouse. She had been locked in. For Talbot, agonized with solicitude, it was equally impossible to emerge from his dressing-room. Further down the passage, Edward Cartaret, interested by this nocturnal manifestation, wrenched and rattled his door-handle in vain.

Muriel, on her silent way through the house to Theodora's bedroom, had turned all the keys on the outside, impartially. She did not know which door might be Edward Cartaret's. Muriel was a woman who took no chances.

THE LAST NIGHT IN THE
OLD HOME

ANNABELLE, who had been searching about upstairs, pinching the corners of mattresses as though they ought to hold guineas and opening and shutting drawers, discovered a pair of gloves in the blue room wardrobe. So she came down to ask everyone whose these could be. From room to room she went: everyone soon learned to dread her step.

'It seems a pity,' she said, 'that they should be sold *with* the wardrobe. They are nice gloves – look.' They were fine suède gloves for narrow hands, worn at the finger-tips, doing up at the wrists with small pearl buttons. 'Someone should have the good of them.'

'Perhaps they're Delia's,' said Henry, her present victim.

'She says no. Hers don't *button* up.'

'I should keep them yourself.'

'Oh, no, Henry, I mustn't; besides, look, they are too small.'

Henry could have screamed. Throughout the house, disappearing in dusk, there reigned an unnatural silence that first he could not account for: all the clocks had been let run down. You cannot auction a ticking clock. The silence echoed, for against the dusty feet of tomorrow all carpets had been rolled up. Here in the morning-room hung a smell of stale notepaper; his mother had taken the family letters – from school, from London, from India – out of the bureau drawers to be read aloud. Now, thank God, they were burnt. Only the best, the jauntiest and most eloquent, had been put away in dispatch cases. All Adrian's had been kept, because he was dead. (With the dispatch-cases no one knew what to do.) Had Henry been dead, his might have acquired some kind of morbid value. As it was, they put up a poor show at the hearing by mother and sisters and had been unostentatiously burnt. Absent or present, he was constrained with his family: too civil, nervous. He was humiliated by Annabelle's oddness, that all the others took calmly. His embarrassment was unforgivable: Annabelle was not 'afflicted'; she simply did not grow up. Inside the big, bustling form of a woman she was a girl of ten. So she remained their home-girl.

After Annabelle, Delia looked into the morning-room. 'How funny it is she said,' briskly, 'with all the pictures down! Smoke had dimmed, sun faded, the wallpaper; fresh flowery squares stared oddly.

Delia always put balm on the rawest of situations by saying something quite brilliantly superficial. She had been clicking round on her high heels, applying this happy touch to the family's nerves, all today and yesterday. Quite beautiful, she had married and left home young: she cared for no one at all. Henry liked her the best of them; she was as gay as a stranger; between these two convention was comfortably present. 'There's a fire,' she said, 'in the library.'

'Who's in there?'

'Mother and father and poor dear John.'

'Doing what?'

'That's the difficulty,' she said brightly; 'there's nothing much they *can* do. Oh, mother is trying to rub out the places where we all used to be measured against the door.'

Something more than her constant wish to be social accounted for Delia's brightness: she felt a profound relief. Something let go of her conscience. Delia was no good; to her husband, who bored her, she had for years been unfaithful; she was as light as a little cat. With home still going on here, some fiction of innocence had always unnerved her. Now mother and father and Annabelle would be people in a hotel; the cuckoo-clock, the scrap screen, the big chintz chairs rumpled by dogs, would all be auctioned tomorrow and carted away. There *it* went — pouf! Its grip relaxed on her spirit ... Delia asked Henry to give her a cigarette, and, balancing with a hand on his shoulder as they stood over the grate cold with papery ashes, she began to tell him, amazingly, all about her life. Once or twice she glanced defiantly round the morning-room. Henry, having had no idea she was such a bad woman, violently registered shock.

She concluded: 'I've always wanted to ask you — do you have love-affairs?'

He looked at her queerly, 'No,' he said.

'How *wise*, but how silly.'

Annabelle went into the kitchen, where cook, for her final credit, was giving a final scrub to the copper and zinc saucepans, then ranging them back in their lots on the dresser and tables. All the other servants had wept and gone. Annabelle turned the handle of the mincing-machine and looked regretfully into a colander. 'Oh, dear,' she sighed. Cook took the mincing-machine firmly away from Annabelle and put it back on a shelf.

'I used to make cakes here, usen't I?'

'You did indeed, miss, and very nice cakes they were. Now let that strainer alone, there's a good girl!'

'Cook, whose gloves *can* these be? No one seems to care.'

No doubt, said cook, they had belonged to a visitor. Her eyes, always watery in their scorched lids from the heat of so many fires, looked smaller and dull, like a dead porcupine's; it was hard to tell if she had been crying. Tomorrow she was going straight on to another gentleman's family. If she felt at all, it was angry sorrow for John. He was her darling: it seemed a direct hit at cook that it should be John who had ruined the family. He had a way with him. He never told cook how much, these days, he detested apricot jam, or that her puddings and cakes made him flatulent.

Decency had required John's presence at the obsequies of the home. He felt this unduly hard; his parents' brave brightness affected him. Their silence from all reproach became sinister, like the silence of clocks. He felt prickly all over and drank a good deal of whisky. When Henry told him, that rationally, this was for the best, that the old place had no place now they were all grown up and there were no grandchildren, and that their parents would do much better out of this valley climate, John became very angry. He felt that it was in spirit Henry who ruined the home. Hard-hit, John felt really innocent. Not once had he been deliberate: if mess-bills ran up, horses he backed turned out rotten, cards he held worthless and women he loved exacting, was John to blame? He told himself he had had no real fun. It had always helped him to think of his old home; after a thick night it made him feel good and squashy.

The marks where the children were measured would not rub off the door; John suggested scratching them out with a pocket-knife, but his mother said that would spoil the paint. So he left the library, where the books were stacked up in lots, and went upstairs to look out of the landing window. Here the garden poplars were visible through the dusk, but he saw more plainly his figure reflected against the sky. He turned from the window; the gas was lit on the landing; outside the nursery door John saw the rocking-horse. So mounted, John as a little fellow had charged impressively, hurling himself on enemies. But, when you got off, those red-painted nostrils

46

were always scoffing away. Maddened, John kicked the rocking-horse.

The rocking-horse, stirrups flying, bumped noisily on its rollers. 'Oh, you *mustn't*!' screamed Annabelle, darting out of the nursery, the suède gloves still in her hand. Kneeling, she crooned on the horse's neck. 'Darling . . . poor darling . . . Wicked, unkind John!'

'Damn!' muttered John, unnerved.

Annabelle heard him. Wild with affront, she scrambled heavily to her feet with a cowlike movement and dashed down the naked stairs. 'Mother, mother,' she wailed. Her mother came out of the library. 'Oh, mother, John said "Damn" to me!'

'Never mind,' said her mother, patting the convulsed home-girl.

'He *looked* so awful.'

'We must be kind to him.'

All the doors were open. Henry and Delia glanced at each other; she smiled at a crease in her sleeve, he fumbled a cigarette out and went quite white. They both felt home had lasted a day too long. John came downstairs; his hand shook on the banisters. He looked in at Delia, mouth twisted as though he wanted to laugh, then pushed past into the dining-room where the decanters were.

'He's right,' said Delia. 'I think I should like one too.'

'Our horse,' Annabelle wailed, 'our old darling horse. . . .'

'This is intolerable,' said Henry. But their mother looked at him with expressionless eyes over Annabelle's heaving shoulder. 'Never mind,' she murmured, and Henry knew that he had been ordered away.

Only the drawing-room, where they were all always polite, remained unentered, untroubled. It was prepared for tomorrow, its last occasion, when crowds would bid for the piano, the sofas, the clock. The rugs were rolled up and numbered, the chairs stood in rows; statues' unwearied arms upheld unlit lamps on the mantelpiece. Twilight came in through the unshuttered windows, hung in drops from the chandeliers, and shone in the mirrors.

A wind came up; creepers began to tap on the south windows; draughts crept through the house, fluttering here and there a ticket on objects already bespoken. A door slammed upstairs. Henry went up to shut the windows; the rocking-horse was still rocking. A straw from some packing-case blew past his feet in the dark, which was melodramatic.

THE DISINHERITED

AUTUMN had set in early. While the days were still glowing, the woods took on from a distance a yellow, unreal sheen, like a reflection from metal; their fretted outlines hardened against the blond open hills that the vibrations of summer no longer disturbed. In the early mornings, dew spread a bright white bloom between long indigo shadows; the afternoon air quickened, but after sunset mists diluted the moon. This first phase of autumn was lovely; decay first made itself felt as an extreme sweetness: with just such a touch of delicious morbidity a lover might contemplate the idea of death.

Later the rain came, and there were drenching monotone days; the leaves, rotting uncoloured, slid down through the rain. Mid-autumn set in mild, immobile and nerveless; the days had unclear margins, mists webbed the gardens all day, the sun slanting slowly through them to touch the brown pear-trees and pale yellow currant-leaves, here and there a marigold or a sodden rose. There was no wind, and the woods stood heavily tense; against their darkness, in the toneless November evenings, the oaks were still yellow and shed a frightening glare. Everything rotted slowly. The dark, rain-swollen rivers flowed fast between bleaching sedges, with leaves caught on the current. After the rain, an unlit grey sky bound the earth, and pools threaded the grass and lay unglittering inside the brittle reeds. Now and then the skies were disturbed by a high-up swift rustling sigh: the summer birds flying south. The shredded last leaves still clung to the trees, as though they would not fall: eternity seemed to have set in at late autumn. Some way into November, a wind sprang up at nights.

Marianne Harvey was not aware of the autumn to which her friend Davina was becoming a prey. Since August, Marianne had been cheerfully busy, without a moment for any kind of reflection; the Harveys were nesting over again, after twelve years of marriage, making a new home. But all those weeks Davina Archworth had been idle with a melancholy and hollow idleness, with all day to kick the wet leaf-drifts and watch the birds go.

The Harveys had left London and come up to live on the new building estate, in a freshly built white rough-cast house with a touch of priggishness in its architecture. The estate, on a hill dominating from some distance a university city, was exclusive; lots here could only be purchased on the distinct condition that houses of a fixed value were to be put up. You undertook not to keep chickens, put up a frame garage or hang out clothes. Into the tone of this niceness the Harveys easily fell. Few houses had gone up so far; those there were stood apart, like Englishmen not yet acquainted, washed by clear upland air and each in its acre of wiry grass that had lost its nature, being no longer meadow and not yet lawn. Half-made roads, like the first knowing cuts of a scalpel, mapped the flank of the hill out, up to the concrete water-tower upon its crest. No buses approached, and there were and would be no shops.

At the foot of this genteel hill, at the river level, the old village frowsted inside its ring of elm-trees, mouldy and snug. Its lichened barn-roofs were yellow, and from the church spire the weathercock now and then shot out one sharp gold ray; from the tower there came up, climbing the hill on Sundays, ponderous chimes. A clot of thin smoke hung melting in watery river light over the roofs of the village; after sunset a few dark lights outlined the three-cornered green. A wide pitch-black by-pass road with white kerbs swept south round the foot of the hill, cutting off the old village from the new building estate. On the far flank of the village the stretching brick-red tentacles of the city made their advance over water-meadows tufted with lines of willow; far off, the brittle city spires pricked at the skyline. The small, shallow river on which the village was built ran into another, grand one: a beetle-green gasometer stood at this point, and there was a steel bridge over which London expresses rumbled and rang. Sometimes a swan, disturbed, sailed up the back-water.

It enraged Davina that the new estate (no affair of her own, as she had not been asked to live there) should not have any shops. Naturally aristocratic, she loathed refinement. She especially liked little shops to be just a minute away from wherever she might be living, shops that are cheesy and mixed and stay open on Sundays, where you buy cigarettes, pepper-mints, shoelaces, picture papers, sardines, purgative pills and writing compendiums with pictures on the outside. She liked chatting late across counters in the dark lamplight and charming unauthorized people into selling her stamps. She had that kind of restless feeling for Marianne that makes one critical; she therefore despised Marianne's habit of shopping by tele-phone, which put her, she thought, out of touch with reality. The whole new estate with its rawness, its air at once hygienic and intellectual, revolted Davina. All the same, she was up there constantly, dropping in at all times of the day to see Marianne Harvey. Attraction, propinquity and, on Davina's part, idleness fostered this funny alliance.

Davina had come to live in the old village with and on her aunt — or, strictly, her uncle's widow — Mrs. Walsingham Archworth. Her existence was temporary; though she had few prospects she was, or had been till lately, hoping for better times. Her aunt's house had been the manor, and Mrs. Archworth, though she had by now disposed of all other property, still looked on herself as patroness of the village. Her house, backed by an ilex and flanked by lines of clipped hollies, had a high, narrow face, with dark inanimate windows, and looked like the frontispiece to a ghost-story. Inside, however, it was kindly, crimson and stuffy. Its front windows looked down a lawn, through wrought-iron gates, on to the village green, where the lime-trees shed their leaves early . . . Davina could not enjoy living here, on her aunt; mortification and dullness ravaged her. But, at twenty-nine, she had no more money of any kind; she had run through her capital; love-affairs and her other expensive habits had ruined her. To earn was out of the question: she had no idea what to do. In an agony of impatience, she waited about indefinitely. Something that should have occurred — she was not sure what — had not occurred yet, and became every day more unlikely. She remained, angry, immobile, regretting that circumstances over which she had had really, at one time, every control, should have driven her into exploiting her aunt's affection.

This was too easy. In looks as well as in temperament Davina resembled her dead uncle, who, melancholy and dashing, had hung up his hat in this house with a gracious despondent gesture and had been loved to distraction by his dull, pink wife throughout the years of their marriage, in return for which he had given her scarcely a smile. Davina herself had, further, just that touch of the sombre romantic about her that appeals to all other women, even to relatives. She was adored by her aunt, now a puffy, huffy, formal, bewildered, charmless elderly widow. Davina was tall, with a head set strikingly on a dark-ivory neck; her springy dark hair, shortish, was tucked back behind her ears. Her features, well cut, were perhaps rather pronounced, but her sombreness and her unwilling smile could be enchanting. She could command that remarkable immobility possible only to nervously restless people, when only her dark eyes' intent and striking glitter betrayed the tension behind. She moved well, with an independent and colt-like carriage; her manner was, for a young woman's, decided, a shade overbearing, intimidating to lovers whom her appearance beguiled. Had she had sphere, space, ease of mind, she might have been generous, active and even noble; emotion need only have played a small part in her life. She was a woman born to make herself felt.

As things were, hurt pride distorted her memories; an inflamed sense of self isolated her; miscarried projects darkened her whole view. Her thoughts were almost all angry. 'If I had money——' she said again and again. She walked miles a day, clicking her third left-hand finger angrily on her thumb, pacing the fields with a long nervy mannish stride. In this countryside she was a stranger; in the mild academic city she cared to know nobody. Friends, it appeared, had forgotten her. Indoors she smoked, kicked the fire up, tore the plots from crime novels, and switched the wireless scornfully on and off.

Mrs. Archworth was sorry to see the hill she had known all her life, and sometimes walked with her husband, cut up for building plots. For several months this had made her huffy, distressed. She had to admit, however, that times were changing, and after some searchings of heart she decided to call on the newcomers. So her heavy Daimler ploughed uphill one afternoon through the mud of the half-made roads, swerving past rubble and bouncing her on the springs. Alas, the new houses were draughty, with sweating plaster, and she returned with a chill: it was unfortunate that she had found anybody at home. Marianne, for her part, had been gratified by Mrs. Archworth's visit, for she took her to be county. It was in returning the call that Marianne had met Davina for the first time: she was shown by the parlourmaid into a morning-room dense with smoke and loud with the wireless, from which Davina, glowering, found no way to escape.

Six days after that, on the ridge of the hill by the water-tower, they met again. Marianne, hatless, was exercising two dogs. Her thick honey-fair hair, ruffling away from her fore-head, glinted in afternoon sunshine that fell on the unspoilt country beyond the hill. Rivery twists of mist lay along the river below. This was the first phase of autumn, the air agitating and sweet. When Marianne saw Davina she blushed with pleasure and shyness. They walked on the skyline, between the brambles that still gave out a morningish smell of dew: Marianna invited Davina back to her house for tea . . . She was house-proud, and led this new friend with a touch of emotion up the path to the porch, across the ambitious raw garden. Davina, however, looked neither to right nor left: indoors, she did give one glance of surprise rather than pleasure round the Harvey living-room, artfully pale and bare, where through steel-framed windows blue-pink afternoon light flooded the walls and waxy expanse of floor. It all looked to Davina nullish, with, here and there, the stigmata of intel-lectual good taste. The hearth was bare, but steam heating drew out sweat from the plaster while, to Davina's senses, devitalizing and parching the air. Ranged round the cold brick hearth, three low chairs with sailcloth cushions invited a confidence everything else forbade. A clock ticked, but the room had no pulse.

'My husband's not here,' said Marianne, looking uncertain. Davina simply said, 'Oh.' They sat down to tea.

'I am fifteen years younger than Matthew,' Marianne said later, apropos of something else.

Matthew had lately retired from the Civil Service owing to ill health. However, he felt better now. At the same time his aunt had died, leaving Matthew more money, so he had decided to live where he liked, and to build. Sentiment had drawn him back to the scene of his happiest years, Marianne having agreed that it would be interesting to live near a university. He was honorary secretary to a society here; in addition to this, he had some philanthropic work in connection with which he was quite often away. He was a member of the senior common-room of his college, and dined in hall three times a term. Once or twice a week the Harveys would dine early and motor into the city to attend the meetings of learned societies or soirées given by the Art Club. Life here was full of interest, Marianne said. Moreover, Matthew and Marianne were happy in each other's affection. After twelve years of marriage his wife still charmed him with her serenity, mild good spirits and love of home. And she had more than this: he took pride in that touch of the farouche about her beauty; she was big-limbed, wide-browed, and looked like a diffident goddess, but her eyebrows turned up to her temples like impatient wings and her alive hair in honey-dark ringlets fell every way. Her fairness and uncertain manner made her seem still quite young: in his friends here she stirred up a dusty sentiment. All this was dear to Matthew, who craved little more than refreshment: he was not a passionate man. Living closely, since they came back here, with the ghost of his own adolescence, raising the old evocations from the same poetry — out of one book slipped a grass-blade twenty-five years old, from another a pressed fritillary — taking the same river- -

walks, he saw how his friends grew greyer, how their senti-
ments creaked, and, with dismay for himself, dreaded to
desiccate. He clung to his wife's ever-freshness, her touch of
the vine-leaf . . . Cautious, well-read, tolerant, and inclined to
be prosy, Matthew had fluffy pepper-and-salt hair thinning
away from the temples, a rather too constant kind smile, and
a nose veined at the bridge; he wore shell-rimmed spectacles
with gold hook-on side-pieces, a Norfolk jacket of antique
cut, and grey flannel trousers that always bulged at the knee.
He and Marianne had two sons, Edwin and Luke; Luke had
just joined Edwin at a preparatory school. When the boys
came back for their first Christmas in the new home they
would be taken for walks by their father, who would describe
his youth here and make them familiar with the antiquities of
the city.

Davina had never learned how a poor relation behaves. She
exacted, grumbled and ordered the servants around, walked
mud into carpets, and stayed in bed overtime, rang bells all
day long, and, till recently took out the car when she chose.
Her aunt's maids admired Davina's lordly habit of being
unfair: their own mistress, with her affronted, muddled and
rather tippeting manner, they had well in control . . . From
the first, however, there had been trouble with the chauffeur.
Prothero, the chauffeur, lived in the coachman's room
above what had been the stables, up a built-in staircase at the
end of the yard. His window faced the Manor back-bedroom
windows. He had been with Mrs. Archworth four months, a
few weeks more than Davina, having been engaged after good
old Robinson died. He had come with a first-rate character;
none of his former employers could write too highly of him.
He was forbiddingly faultless, a careful driver; he did not
grumble, make love to the maids or expect beer. Mrs. Arch-

worth could never be certain why she did not like him better, or why his proximity while he was tucking her into the car, his way of receiving orders, even the set of his shoulders and back of his ears as he drove, should fill her with a resentful uneasiness. There was something unlikely about him and she mistrusted the odd. Between his flat peaked blue cap and his blue collar his face was always shadowless, abstract, null; a face remembered as being unmemorable. The only look he gave you was level and unmoving. Though she got all she paid for, she could not feel he was hers. Her cook was 'my cook', but he remained 'the chauffeur'. His manner had not that alacrity to which she was accustomed; always on the polite side of surly, he was at the same time unsmiling and taciturn. Here, however, he was, and she dreaded change as in some way an ally of death . . . So that she liked to think his oddness was simply his surname; such an unusual name for a chauffeur, everyone said.

But one point against Prothero Mrs. Archworth *could* fix: he burnt light too late. Her own nights were often disturbed by a windy form of dyspepsia; her long bedroom extended the depth of the house, and it was annoying to see, through the blind of her back window, Prothero's light still burning, behind the screen of the ilex, till one or two o'clock. It became her nervous habit to court the annoyance, to wake again and again to see if this were still so. Mrs. Archworth would lie rigid with anger and speculation. Finally, one morning, flushing with apprehension, she protested against this use of her electricity. Prothero bowed. That night, at ten o'clock, he flicked off his hanging light with sardonic promptness: a dimmer glow succeeded: he sat up by candle-light. She had to suppose, with an obscure sense of frustration, the candles might be his own. Night after night, as she still peered through the ilex, not a shadow moved on his

blind. She suspected him, all the same, of bringing in women
— but the yard gates were bolted and there was never a sound
from the dog.

His life at the edge of this household of women remained
inscrutable. But one thing they could all see: he could not do
with Davina. She would take out the car when it pleased her,
without a word to Prothero: she brought it in always dirty
and sometimes late. Then one night she had found the gates
bolted against her; two days after that he had locked the
garage. Davina went, stormy, for Prothero. No one knew
what occurred, but after that she no longer took out the car.
No word from either side reached Mrs. Archworth direct.
During this friction between her niece and her chauffeur
she behaved like a terrified ostrich. After that week, things
had quieted down for a bit.

One night in early November, Prothero, in reply to a
whistle repeated on a rising note and each time with less
caution, opened his door at the head of the built-in staircase
and came half-way down, cigarette in his mouth. The stairs
creaked as he padded, and came to a stop silently. Davina
stood in the arch at the foot of the staircase, with Marianne
Harvey behind her out in the yard. Their figures were
silhouetted against a patch of yard lamplight. Both the
young women were hatless and wore heavy overcoats.
Against the night sky, clotted and dense, the papery ilex
shivered; night wind, with a sinister flitter of dead leaves,
raced round the yard, whose cobbles dappled away into
leathery bat's-wing darkness beyond the lamp.

The two stood looking up; the staircase creaked again, and
Prothero still said nothing. Davina advanced with a nervous
swaggering movement and put one foot on the stairs. She
began: 'Look here——'

He said uncivilly: 'Well?'

She dug her hands into her pockets. 'I want some more money,' she said with a casual air.

He shifted his cigarette. 'What,' he said, '*now?* Tonight?'

'Naturally,' said Davina, with some impatience. Outside the archway Mrs. Harvey stepped back and glanced uneasily round her into the dark, as though she did not care at all for her company. An unseen smile hung in the dark of the stairs; Prothero let his cigarette drop and ground it out with his heel. 'For heaven's sake,' she said, '*hurry*'; and shifted her foot. The deliberate and endless silence was painful to Marianne. 'Right,' he said. 'Come on up.'

He turned back into his room, and Davina, with automatic swiftness and energy, went springing upstairs after him. His door stayed ajar; vibrations of heat from the stove came down through the arch to the horrified Marianne. Looking up at the dark sky, she fought for a feeling of everybody's nonentity. The clock in the church tower, not far away, struck nine: before the last stroke finished Davina was down again. She caught Marianne by the elbow and ran her across the yard. They paused by the lamp a minute; Davina held a crackling note close up to Marianne's face. 'That is that,' she said.

Wincing away from the note, with its smell of delinquency, Marianne, not for the first time, wished herself safe at home. But the wish was the merest moment's frightened retraction and not sincere: Marianne's heart was set on this evening's pleasure, this fantastic setting-out. In these weeks of knowing Davina her faculty for disapproval seemed to be all used up. She was under a spell. She blamed herself, and knew Davina despised her, for being too shy or too sly to ask Matthew for money before he started for London, where he would stay tonight.

She said faintly, 'Oh, how you *could* . . .'

Her friend looked satirical. She had seen Marianne's recoil from the servant's money. On the subject of class, she knew, Marianne felt as awkwardly and obscurely as people do about sex. Marianne said: 'But why not go to your aunt?'

'You have no idea of what's impossible and what's not! It would make *me* sick to ask Matthew—— However, that's your affair. Now, for God's sake, my good girl, don't waste any more time!'

Marianne's brain hummed with frightening anticipation. Leaving the yard, they crept like a couple of cats round the unlit flank of the house, between the wall and the spiny flutter of hollies. Round at the front, an inch-wide slit of bright light fell on Davina's smile: secrecy quickened their breath as they stopped a minute to look in between the drawing-room curtains at Davina's aunt at bridge with three of her neighbours. In the dense red-shaded lamplight sealed in by the pane the two ladies' lace jabots, the two gentlemen's shirt-fronts, stood out like tombstones: the intent quartette, the glazed cabinets and woolly white rugs, all looked embedded in something transparent, solid and hot, like clarified red wax. Not a sound came through the pane. The two turned and crept away down the dark lawn.

Outside the gates, Marianne's coupé had been run up on to the rough grass of the green, with its lights out. Its air was lurking and crookish. They got in, and Marianne ran the car bumpily off the grass and away down a lane between blank end-walls of cottages, on to the by-pass road. Marianne's heart went up as they slid clear of the walls that had stared amazed in her headlights: the sweeping black irresistible river of road sucked at her will like a current; their speed heightened; with a swing of lights they swept south. Davina eyed the speedometer. 'Hurry,' she said.

Marianne had a flicker of spirit. 'If you bully me, I'll go home.'

'Let me *drive*——'

'No.'

'Oh, very well, Mrs. Harvey.'

'This is a good beginning,' said Marianne, sore.

'Left!' said Davina sharply, and held to the lights of the dashboard, as they approached a cross-roads, a vague little pencilled map. After some minutes she said: 'If it makes you feel any better, he's not a chauffeur; he's a crook.'

'Don't be silly,' said Marianne. An impassable wall of good humour divides any lady from fact. But she could not resist saying, 'Besides, how do you know?'

'I know he knows I know. He's lying low here. I've seen his photograph somewhere — something once happened.'

'You get ideas in your head from reading those frightful books.'

'But things do happen, you know,' said Davina calmly. Sliding down in her seat and eyeing the flying darkness, she fingered the note in her pocket with cautious pleasure, like someone hugging a thought. Meanwhile Marianne thought of a smart little Jewish girl she used to go to tea with when she was nine years old and living at Dulwich. That little girl had declared there was a dead baby strapped up in a trunk in her family's cistern loft. After tea in the frightening Gothic house, they had crept up to the door, but Marianne would not go in, hearing with horror the cistern inside gurgle. But later her mother told her the little Jewish girl was not a lady, and ever since then Marianne had thought of the extraordinary with contempt. Pressing her chin down in the folds of her muffler, she made up her mind to ask no more about Prothero.

Prothero's pound note was soon changed, for Marianne

had not filled up the car and they had to pull up for petrol: she ran the car into the bay of a filling station. While the man unlocked the pump, Marianne got out a minute, restlessly, from the car. Behind them, the last lights of streets were strung along the horizon; the thin glow above a provincial city hung on the sky. Marianne felt her face turned for ever to the unknown. But flight was life to Davina, with nothing to leave behind.

A friend's unknown friends are daemons or demigods with frightful attributes. Marianne's heart sank at the thought of the meeting ahead. The night air was uncalming and anxious: no moon but a rolling hurry of clouds: a circle of rotting flower-stalks outside the petrol station shivered under their headlights in the dark wind.

They drove on.

A glittering Neon sign like wolves' eyes read: OPEN ALL NIGHT, at which thought a dry weariness pervaded the brain. 'We shan't be staying *all* night,' said Davina easily. Here they were, and they tore up the pencilled map and scattered the scraps on the wind.

The road-house stood at the cross-roads, its row of Christmas-card windows shedding a fictitious glow. Four wide black roads had been levelled into the hill, and met in a kind of circus inside the clay banks of the cutting. The road-house stood high up; to the porch you mounted some steps up the high embankment; a car park was scooped out fifty yards further on. The wind moaned cheerlessly over the down behind, but the scene had a hard air of late night merriment, like a fixed grin . . . In the porch, Marianne pulled off a gauntlet to tuck back a strand of hair; Davina whipped out her lipstick and gave herself new, bright lips. 'We were once rather in love.'

But inside there was no one. A long row of swinging lanterns bobbed in their own horrid light as they pushed open the door. The lounge was empty and bald as the inside of a band-box, glazed with synthetic panelling. The chairs were askew, empty, with flattened cushions; ashtrays sent up a cold fume; the place wore an air of sudden, sheepish vacuity, as though a large party had just got up and gone out. The barman leaned, yawning, just inside the bar shutter. When they came in, he took no notice. Davina's friends had not come.

Davina, who had sauntered in with a smile on her fine reddened lips, dropped the smile and looked round her, utterly at a loss.

'Perhaps we are early,' said Marianne.

'No.'

'Perhaps they are late?'

'They can't be later than us.'

'Perhaps they've given us up?'

'They know I am always late——' Davina broke off, crossed the room, and angrily questioned the barman. No, no one had asked for her; no one had waited; no one had telephoned. Sitting down by the shutter, she snapped out an order for bitter. 'I can't drink beer,' said Marianne, as it was brought.

'You'd better,' Davina said with a hollow look.

Marianne fingered her glass. 'This seems a funny place to be meeting anyone in. . . .'

'Well, we're not, you see. Does that make it all right?'

A clock struck ten; someone bumped down the bar shutter and locked it. The barman came for their glasses. So that was that.

After some time Marianne said: 'You know, we can't wait all night.'

'I don't see why not.'

Lighting a cigarette, Davina said no more. An uneasy silence set in. Marianne, watching her friend's lips pulling at the cigarette, the once bold dark eyes that now crept to the door then dropped quickly to cover their mortification, felt pity go through her heart with a shameful pang. She also was mortified, and could have easily wept. She only half knew now all she had hoped of tonight. Girlish delicious expectancy went sour inside her. She was tragically sold. She had been, from the first, imposed on by something about Davina — her dashingness, curtness and air of experience. In these last weeks, Marianne's consciousness had been extended deliciously, painfully. A segment of bright unknown world had fallen across her path, where it shed prisms. Only she knew what formless excitement had racked her lately.

But where was Tonight?

Seeing Davina sitting, so much at a loss, with 'Forgotten' pasted across her, too proud to look up, Marianne felt the world contract again. In the next room, someone put a wailing blues on the gramophone. Marianne wished she were home, with her feet on the hot pipes and the cat on her stomach. Out here, draughts raced round the floor.

Davina shot up and said: 'I shall telephone!'

.   .   .   .

They drove on again. 'I'll tell you one thing,' Davina was saying. 'Somebody's double-crossed me. Unless Oliver's lying — and I don't think he'd be lying — I ought to have got his message at aunt's today.'

'Plans are changed?' quavered Marianne.

'Yes, don't you *see*——' said Davina. Her spirits, however, were up. She sat smiling and silent, looking along the headlights. Things had changed for the better. They had swung east at the cross-roads, always further from home. After more miles of flying hypnotic night, Davina said it ought to be anywhere now. 'Any time now, on your right...' On their right, they crept in between two Palladian lodges, unlit and staring, the wide gates standing apart. Beech-trunks raced past their lights and a sleek wettish avenue spattered under the tyres: three more gates were hooked back.

The immense façade of the house rushed glaring on to their headlamps: between high white-shuttered windows pilasters soared out of sight above an unlit fanlight like patterns of black ice. Reaching across Marianne, Davina touched the horn, which sent up that face of coldness its peevish cry. The cry repeated — 'They can't even *hear!*' she groaned. But then the fanlight amazingly sprang into light, the hall door burst open on a perspective of pillars, and, with so much thrusting and force that this seemed a muffled riot, dark people shot out, surrounded the car, and pulled open both doors at once. Marianne ducked in a sweep of night air. Davina, peering, said: 'Oliver?'

'I've g-got this all to myself!' exclaimed an excitable voice.

'Where's Thingummy?'

'O-o-oh, he never turned up.'

'So he's not here,' said a woman.

'I am furious,' said Davina.

'That's too bad,' said Oliver, pulling Davina out of the car with a glass in his other hand. 'Never mind, you're here now.'

'It was too bad,' agreed someone. 'However, here we all are.'

They trooped back into the hall. A stout, speechless man who had pulled Marianne through the other door of the car looked at her in the light, closely, to see what he had got.

He seemed satisfied. Indoors, the immense cold hall, all chequered pavement and pillars, wore an air of outrage, ravished by steps and voices. One door stood open, and light peered in at the glacial sheeted outlines of furniture and a chandelier that hung in a bag like a cheese and glittered inside the muslin. A chill came from the hearthstones; the house was masterless. Along a pathway of drugget over the marble, at a quick muffled shuffle as though conducting a funeral secretly, the revellers passed down the hall to a door at the far end. They shot through with a rush, each unwilling to be the last, and shut the door defiantly on the echoing house.

'Outside there gives you the creeps,' said the only woman who spoke. Davina's friend Oliver, dishevelled, fair, aquiline, and unnaturally tall, turned and shook hands with Marianne. 'I didn't see you,' he said. 'I'm so glad you came. I hope you had no trouble; I went down just now and opened the gates myself. Do you know if the sheep got out? · They are grazing sheep; things are not what they used to be.'

Smoke and human stuffiness thickened the air of this room with its dead undertone of chill on which a snapping wood fire had little effect. It was a high, shabby, gilt-and-white octagonal ante-room, the naked shutters of three windows fortified by iron bars. Bottles crowded a top-heavy ornate table under the chandelier; panels of tarnished mirror kept multiplying the company, and on a red marble column a Psyche balanced with one hand over a breast. Oliver said: 'I brought her in here for company: I always liked the girl.' On a settee, pulled across the hearth at an angle, an enormous congested old lady slept with her feet apart, letting out stertorous breaths. Her wool coatee was pinned over the heaving ledge of her bust with a paste brooch in the form of a sailing-ship, and at each breath this winked out a knowing

66

ray. Her hands, chapped and knouty, lay in the trough of her lap. Half under her skirts a black pair of kitchen bellows lay on the marble fire-kerb. There was not much more furniture in the room.

'That is Mrs. Bennington, who takes care of me. She's so nice,' said Oliver. He rinsed a glass out at a siphon and brought Davina a drink. 'It's a nice house, too,' he said, 'till you get used to it.'

'It's all right once one's got here. Why not suggest this

'You see, I thought there'd be Thingummy.'

'Well, you certainly muddled things,' said Davina with less rancour, her nose inside her glass. When he and she had been younger, handsome, high-spirited, and still with some-thing to spend, they had been in love, and expected to marry one day. Their May had been blighted. Now, each immobile from poverty, each frozen into their settings like leaves in the dull ice of different puddles, they seldom met. They had the dregs of tenderness left for each other, but, each time they met, less to say. It was best to meet in a crowd, as they met tonight. Tonight the crowd was not large, but things might have been worse.

Oliver shook the dregs from another glass and absently rinsed it, meanwhile looking at Marianne. He said to Davina: 'Will she enjoy herself?'

'She has a deadly life. Her standard is not high.'

'She looks most beautifully shy,' Oliver said wistfully.

Marianne felt very shy. The more the room settled down, the more strongly she felt she had no place here. She stood with a hand on the mantelpiece, looking blindly about with her wide-apart troubled eyes. The stout man who had her in charge snatched the glass Oliver had been so vaguely holding, filled it, and brought it to Marianne. 'Now you'll feel better,' he said. His name was Purdon. Marianne could not explain that she did not like whisky. The smell of spirits repelled and interested her; her nostrils quivered; she drank. '*That's* better,' said Purdon, and bustled up with a chair. Marianne sat down blinking and holding her glass. As though she had been a refugee, her coming in had seemed to constitute some kind of emergency.

'Where are we?' she said.

'Ah, *that's* just the fun,' said Purdon. 'Where we've no call to be!'

'As much call as anyone else,' said the platinum blonde oldish girl, Miriam. She knelt by the kerb and, pulling the bellows from under Mrs. Bennington's skirts, began to puff at the fire. She coaxed the flames up knowingly; firelight flapped on her face and up Marianne's knees. An un-English man in a crimson high-necked pullover reached his drink from the floor and resettled himself on the settee, one arm around Mrs. Bennington, with an air of content. These were all the people there really were in the room. The party resumed its tenor, illicit but not defiant. A low-spirited intimacy, an innocent kind of complicity, made itself felt. Little seemed worth saying, everything understood. What was said strayed up like bubbles from depths of interiority. They had the flat, wise air of a party of bandit children with their bravado put off, gathering in a cellar.

Marianne looked into her glass; where had all that gone? Her dilated eyes swam round the smoky gilt-and-white room with its tarnished reaches of mirror. She met Oliver's look that was like something swimming desperately on a heaving tide of light. Her throat pricked and she pulled at the scarf she still wore. She exclaimed to the fat man: 'This is nicer than where we were!'

'More homey?' he said nicely. She let him unwind her

scarf and drape it about the Psyche. 'That poor girl,' he said, 'gives me the shivers.'

'It feels homey all right to me,' said Miriam, withdrawing her head from the grate. She wiped bellows-black from her fingers on to her black velvet skirt and went on: 'Which may throw some light on my pedigree, now that I come to think.'

No one knew who her father was; he might have been almost anyone. Owing her unkind and scandalous mother no duty, Miriam was always glad to air this uncertainty: it gave her a feeling of space and sometimes, to her mind, a slightly divine quality. She was herself a shady and bitter very good-hearted girl whom everyone liked and nobody seemed to want.

All Oliver's friends were like this. He was, like Davina, an enemy of society, having been led to expect what he did not get. His father had sold himself up and Oliver had had from him little but bad advice. Oliver despised the rich and disliked the poor and drank to the bloody extinction of the middle classes. He wished to call no man brother, and disbelieved with ferocity in himself. The old order left him stranded, the new offered him no place. He lived as he could, and thought well of Davina for settling herself on her aunt. His own relations had, under the suavity of their aspect, a mean kind of canniness, and were not to be imposed upon: they did what they could by imposing him on their friends. Perverse bad manners and clumsiness disqualified Oliver for the profession of being a guest, by which otherwise he might have victualled and housed himself. He had once or twice, on his uncle's recommendation, catalogued country-house libraries; his work was impatient, showy and incorrect, but no one had said so so far, for fear of offending his uncle. He was an ungracious beggar, and, handicapped by a stammer, uncertain health and excitable sensibility, an embarrassment to himself. With his height and fairness he was, in an overcast kind of a way, magnificent-looking: a broken-spirited Viking. He was capable of fantastically disinterested affections. Not having been born for nothing into a privileged class, he was, like Davina, entirely unscrupulous.

Lord Thingummy — so Oliver called him, and it is good enough for the purposes of this tale — possessed a fine, mouldy, unreadable library. Inflated, one night at his club, by intellectual pride, he had let himself be persuaded by Oliver's uncle as to the existence, down at his house in the country, of possible unknown treasures in calf and vellum, and induced to hire Oliver to explore and catalogue these. For this he gave Oliver twenty pounds and his victuals. Lord Thingummy had been disposed to join Oliver for a few days in the country; but yesterday he had wired to put off. The very thought of the place had been too damp for him. His caretaker, Mrs. Bennington, was put in charge of Oliver, with instructions not to make him too comfortable, for one had heard of Oliver as a dilatory chap . . . Lord Thingummy was thus, tonight, the party's unconscious host.

The man on the settee in a crimson pullover was a White Russian with little stake in the future. Tonight he was on a holiday; as a rule he lived rather drearily with a woman of means who had a feeling for Russians, in a maisonette just off Addison Road. Miriam was a girl he and Oliver knew. The stout man, Purdon, was a dentist who had won five thousand pounds in an Irish Sweep and shut up his surgery till this should all be spent: he regretted nothing. Tomorrow he went back to work. He was overflowing with friendliness and had bought the drinks for tonight.

Thingummy, said Oliver, was so damned mean he had had the heating turned off and taken the key of the cellar. The library, where he had said he had no doubt Oliver would be happy browsing about, smelt of must. 'He had the n-nerve,' said Oliver, 'to send me down here to live on chops in this ice-house. May his soul rot like his books!'

Purdon explained to Marianne by what a remarkable stroke of luck they all came to be here. When she understood, she had only one thought: she was agonized — the angry earl would appear. Her brain stopped like a clock; she had met few peers. She said unsteadily: 'I must be going home.'

'Rats,' said Purdon. Nobody else heard.

Davina and Oliver pulled cushions on to the parquet and sat with their shoulders against a corner of the settee. She said: 'How is the catalogue?'

'Getting on fast; I'm so anxious to get away.'

'Where shall you go next?'

'How should I know?'

'You might come and stay with my aunt.'

'That would depend,' he said. 'I must have a look at her first.'

Miriam tittered: 'He's put in the names of the stuck-on books on the doors.'

'He's as likely to read those as any others,' said Oliver.

Marianne trembled and stood up, eyeing her empty glass. She thought: 'Where am I?' put down her glass, and began to finger her way along the mantelpiece's swags and medallions. She thought the marble throbbed. In despair, she sat carefully down again, gripping the scrolled gold chair-arms. Looking across for Davina, she met Oliver's eyes once more. He immediately got up and came to her side. 'I've forgotten your name,' he said.

'Marianne,' she said. 'But I've got to be going home.'

He exclaimed in distress: 'Aren't you happy?'

She hesitated. 'I feel lost.'

'Why do you say that?' said Oliver miserably.

71

Her uncertain look turned away from him to the fire; he saw her cheeks burn and her trembling, obstinate grip on the arms of the chair. Feeling unutterably misspent and guilty, he turned and said to Davina: 'Don't let her go!'

'She's worn out,' said Davina, 'naturally.' Mortification came flooding back to her; she plucked angrily at a carnation she had taken from one of her aunt's vases and stuck in her buttonhole. 'That place was awful,' she said. '*You* simply thought, "No doubt they'll turn up here somehow." Message? I got no message. You seem to expect one to know where you are by instinct! People like you waste one's life!'

'Your aunt ought to be on the telephone.'

'You just hate trouble,' she said.

'Well, don't make it,' said Oliver.

'Please don't quarrel,' said the Russian. Their angry dialogue took place across the room. Through some seconds of silence Mrs. Bennington wheezed.

'I took the message,' said Miriam, 'I, in my little fly – I mean, in my little car: I took the message. Purdon and I drove up to your aunt's house on the way from buying the drink. We snooped around the front lawn and just felt we couldn't face it, so we went round to the back and you still weren't there. They said you weren't anywhere. So we left word with a man who was polishing up a Daimler—'

'That is so,' said Purdon. 'We left word with the chauffeur.'

'We left word very particularly,' said Miriam. '*Don't* come where we said, we said, come straight to Thingummy's, here, because he's not here, so we can be. We even drew you a map,' said Miriam earnestly.

Davina pulled the carnation to pieces. 'I'd like to believe you,' she said, 'but I got no message.'

'Then somebody double-crossed you,' said Miriam.

By half-past ten Mrs. Archworth's evening was over. The parlourmaid let out the retired Indian Civilian and his wife and the retired admiral, who pattered away round the green, with its dim lamps, to their cottages past the church. In the drawing-room the parrakeet, disturbed by the sudden silence, fidgeted under its red baize cover. Mrs. Archworth turned two of the lamps out and stooped for a good night chat with the Pekinese. The parlourmaid came in to take out the tray of glasses.

'Shall I shut up, madam?' she said.

'Not till Miss Davina is in. She is dining at Mrs. Harvey's; she won't be late. No doubt they will see her home. You must leave the door on the latch and come down later to bolt it.'

Kissing the Pekinese between the eyeballs, Mrs. Archworth handed it over regretfully to the parlourmaid; she picked up her lozenge-box, her patience cards, and a paper-knife, and, with her usual air of unfocused indignation — for she seldom expected to sleep — went up to bed. The parlourmaid followed her up with a glass of hot water. Shaking her nightly powder into the glass and watching the water cloud, the aunt awaited, on the stretch and uneasy, Davina's step on the gravel. Outside two red rings of lamplight the darkness showed flat and empty; her thoughts groped around in it ignorantly, like tentacles, asking what everybody was doing, where everybody might be. She did not regret, however, that she was not on the telephone. Her axiom had been always: People can come to see one, or else people can write.

At ten o'clock to the minute Prothero lit four candles stuck into bottles and with satiric promptness flicked out the hanging light. So that Mrs. Archworth, peering out later through her back window-curtains, found his blind pallid.

73

His room, a manservant's, with match-boarded ceiling, glazed cotton blind and fibre matting, was bare; the furniture showed by candlelight mean outlines on the whitewash. The man had no belongings; the place seemed to be to let. His chauffeur's tunic hung huddled against the back of the door. The stove through its mica front shed a dull red glow on the matting. The wind had dropped; inside its walls and high locked gates the yard down there was as still and deep as a well. Not a draught stirred those thin sheets of close-written paper shuffled over his table. Reaching the four candles closer to his left elbow, he went on writing again.

His hand with the twitching pen went rushing from line to line at a fever-high pace. He did not once pause. The pen rushed the hand along under some terrific compulsion, as though something, not thought, vital, were being drained out of him through the point of the pen. Words sprang to their places with deadly complicity, knowing each other too well . . . Once or twice when a clinker fell in the stove, or the outside staircase unaccountably creaked as though a foot were upon it, he looked up, the tyrannic pen staggered, he looked round the room with its immutable fixtures as though he were a ghost—

— grave to the N.N.E. of the church tower in the sunk bit by the wall. No stone yet as it's too soon, the earth is too soft, but a wire wreath frame left with some stalks of some sort of flowers, they were quite dead. Last month you must have got soaked through to what was your heart, rain comes hard on a grave with the earth not set yet. So now you must do without company. I went once.

You said once you thought you should like to die in a ward, for company. As much as you thought, you thought that. Well I was there. But you never thought much of that.

Whatever you did want it wasn't that, whatever you did want you didn't seem to be getting. I never did know what you did want and I don't think you did. What you did get you didn't want, that was me. But you got what you didn't want. You got that and now I don't want any more.

I don't want you any more because I don't want any more. I don't want more of all that so I don't want you or see you. I don't see your eyes that you thought as much as you thought I should not forget. If you could think now you could not think how much I never want you and how much I forget. I don't go back to the bungalow. If you could see you could see how much I forget that time. You could see I don't see the picture of dogs' heads and the pink dotted curtain flapping or standing still or the moth bumping round the whole time or the magazine with the girl's face by your feet on the bed. You tried with eyes to say I should always see them but you were wrong. They are in a list, I can say them but I can't see them.

The bungalow is shut up, the papers call it a love nest but what you got there does no good to that kind of place. No woman would go there now and no one but a fool woman would have gone there in the first place. You said that yourself first thing when I came, it was no good, it was mouldy, the trees drip on the roof and over the edge of the roof, that made green smears, the press was musty inside where you hung your dress and it was you said the sheets had a musty smell. If you wanted to be by the river you should have been by the river and not a field off, and then that might not have been such a lonely place. For all I know no one goes there and as I do not see it it may not be there, for all I know.

Now I don't want all that any more, now I don't want, I get on fine here with no more ants in my brain. The old woman's all right. She gets what she wants. I shut her into the hearse, it is like a hearse, with her rug and her dog and we go bumping along. My ears stick out like you said under my cap and the buttons have crests, a fist with a knife, and I click my heels when she talk‑ I give satisfaction here if you know what that means but you do not know what that means. She gets her money's worth.

I always was what I am, now I am what I always was, what you said that time. Flunkey. I like what I am, a free man. Up here I'm as snug as a monk with a stove with two hours' fuel, no pictures, no pictures of dogs. The bed squeaks when I turn so I lie still like you lie, only it's broader, with your arms down at your sides. My stairs are my stairs and no one comes up, if I did want they would come. I have that money you had, that was my money you had, a bad debt after all I did. The girl owes me seven pound ten and six, so I buy the kisses now. All the fun's in the deal now I know what I don't want.

They say when you've done what I've done you go back. But that's not true. I went once where you are to be sure you are there, but I don't go where we were that last time. I don't act any way they would think I would act. I act my own way now, only I act that way because it is my way. If I don't know what I will do, how can they know what I will do? I act now before I think, and I don't think after I act. I act how I like. You always knew what I would do, so I always had to do that. Now no one knows, I don't know, I act.

Love was just having to act in the one way. There was just one way we could go, like both being in a tram. We acted the way we had to. Slippings-off just us two and fake names and quarrels and all that fun. They all go that same way. Where the tram didn't take the points, where the bump was, was your way with that money you had. You had all the money. The clink in your gold chain bag that you always watched and always kept by your hand and the wallet you brought out when the

bills came, smiling because it was you had the money to spend
but not liking to spend your money and smiling at me that
knowing way and pushing the notes back that we didn't want
yet. You could pay for the fancies you had with all that money
you had. Our bed smelt of all your money. I was a fool then
to love you the way I did, I gave more than you paid for, you
saw I was a fool and that you paid for a fool. You were not
the big business man's daughter for nothing, Anita, and not
the great big business man's wife.

No one saw so no one knew, we met first of all in the train
so no one knew we had met, we didn't write letters, you were
very smart that way, you were very sly. I saw you were no
good. Your husband was a strict man. For some time we
tricked your husband all over the place in a hurry, then you
said there was no time, we had to have more time, we had to
have some place. What with being so plotty, so damned
smart, so careful no one would see us who would remember,
a different place every time — that was not value, you thought.
You had to have more time, you said. What did you have to
have more time for? You'd torn me up by that time, in that
first month, what more did you want? You went off and
leased that bungalow in a fake name. By that time I was
poison to you, and you were to me. It rained that first day
that was the last time, when you told me I had to come there.
I left my car in the garage outside the town up the river and
then I walked down in the rain to where you were. I felt like
lead, the wind bent the trees back on the hill on the far side,
the rain hit the river, it was all dark grey like a photograph.
No one was out, I didn't meet anyone. I felt like a stone.
When I came round the trees I saw that was the place and I
hated the place with trees dripping on the roof and streaks on
the white gate. It looked a hole for a toad. When I came up
the path a window blew open, a pink dotted curtain blew out

in the wet. Your arm came out after the curtain and shut the window so I knew you were in there waiting. The trees up there lashed about. You had seen me, of course. Then, at that time, I couldn't see any way out. There was no air in the house. Though the place was alone with nobody going by you drew the pink curtain as soon as I came in. The whole time the windows rattled, the rain got lashed down by the trees on our roof.

At sunset the wind stopped and then the rain stopped, I got up and opened the window. There was a yellow light near the river, it was hot because it was July, now the wind had stopped, and then everything steamed. The steam made everything hot, moths came out and bumped on the windows as it was getting darker, musty smells came out of the walls of the room where we were. We were done in by then. You began crying and I went off to open a can of corned beef to eat. I shut the door but you opened it, you went on talking at me while I was opening the can and that note came in your voice like the needle skidding on the inside of a record when the record is done. When I didn't answer you came into the kitchen the way you were and asked for a cigarette. I said I hadn't a cigarette, I'd been looking for yours. Then you said what you said. So I went out and walked.

I walked along by the river and didn't meet anyone, I thought I wouldn't go back but my hat was there and you had to have some answer to what you had said. I saw you had me bought up. A motor salesman who didn't do big business and didn't have money and started to have tastes he didn't have money for. A war gentleman after the war, you'd have liked me then in the war. I could see how things were. A man with the sort of face everybody forgot, that you said you mostly forgot. I walked some time by the same bit of the river. I didn't go far.

When I came back you had lit the lamp by the bed and lay smoking and reading a magazine with a girl's face on the front, you knew I would come back. I came and stood the other side of the lamp to wait till you had finished your magazine story. You stretched your arms past your head and yawned and arched up your back, then you smiled the way you smiled and said you'd been nervous. You said how much you liked company, like you had always said. But when I didn't say anything but just waited, without noticing you, you turned over slowly as though you were so comfortable and slid your hand slowly between your cheek and the pillow and said that again slowly. You said that again. You said what you meant. You said what you'd said before. I saw a red mist where your face was, just a mist on the pillow. I took the pillow and smothered you.

The moth bumped about the whole time I leaned on the pillow, then flew into the curtain. The picture of dogs' heads was over the bed and the magazine stayed by your feet on the bed, when you didn't move any more it was still there. Your eyes were looking at me when I lifted the pillow. I took the note-case out of your gold handbag and took your pearls off the table and took your rings and I left the lamp by you to burn out. I left fingerprints, I suppose. I took no trouble. I had taken trouble enough. I banked on no one knowing I knew you. I rubbed your face powder off the mirror with my elbow and had a good look, I thought at least I'd remember my own face. I went out leaving the door on the latch. You stayed there, that was all you knew. You stayed alone.

I took the gold bag that you always kept by your hand and dropped it in the river along the bank. Clouds came up again but everything was quite quiet, it was dark then. Walking away for always from where you were I didn't feel like me yet. Two swans went by but I didn't meet anyone by the river. It was past ten, I came to the town with the garage, I passed the cinema then, they were all coming out. I joined in with them all and walked to the garage along with some people, we all took our cars out. I drove south towards New-haven, and pulled up the car by a wood and slept for a bit, then I drove on. I put up the car at Newhaven when it was light and crossed by the day boat the way it had been arranged. I was crossing to France that day on the firm's business anyhow. In Paris I sold your pearls and two of your rings, I kept the third I liked best. I was at Le Mans when I saw they'd found you, then the firm sent me on to Lyons and I saw your face in the papers, you were the bungalow crime, the French papers had you in because you were young and pretty and it looked like a man. It seemed funny to think I knew you when I saw you in those papers. Your husband covered our tracks, he thought more of being so strict than of hanging anybody, he was just like you always said. He said you'd taken the bunga-low for yourself for a rest cure and he had been going to join you. That didn't help the police so they fixed robbery for the motive and pulled in a tramp but the finger-prints didn't fit, then they went after a deserter from Aldershot, they're not so sharp as they say. For all everyone knew I might not have been born.

This seemed odd to me, when I knew for the first time I had been born and knew who I was now. I felt grand those weeks and fit to lift a ton weight with nothing to lift but pennies. I felt so grand I didn't know what to do. I was all alone. I didn't get thick with anybody for fear of talking when there was only the one thing I wanted to tell anybody. My head stayed very good and I saw the sense of things I never had seen the sense of. Everything got simple. So I began to like life and want a run for my money, else what was the good of being the way I was? So I wasn't taxing my good luck any

THE DISINHERITED

more, I thought I would stage a get-out and start new, the chance came when the firm sent me to Marseilles. Mutts disappear there every day.

A man came along there that was what I wanted, a drunk, Prothero, a chauffeur who'd been sacked from a villa near Antibes, he'd drunk all his money in Marseilles, he was so tight he sold me his passport for two hundred francs and threw in his references for fifty more. His face fitted mine all right I said if he'd meet me again I'd give him the fifty francs that I hadn't on me the first time: he turned up blind again. I walked him down by the quays where there weren't so many lamps and then nudged him over into the harbour, he wasn't giving a damn for what happened next anyhow, so that was all right by him, he sank like a stone. I went back to his place and checked out his luggage, I left mine where it was in my hotel. The hotel people reported me missing, they found my papers and passport along with my luggage and wrote back to the firm. I wasn't just then owing the firm anything, so they didn't worry, they concluded I'd been one more of those fool English who get themselves done in in the pleasure quarter and aren't heard of again. The French police poked round but they get sick of the English. I hadn't any family to make trouble, nobody cared so everyone let things drop. My photograph was in the French papers and in the English papers, and it must have been funny for people to think they had known me. No one remembered my face. No one went into mourning, no one felt that way. After a bit I came back to England and began to put Prothero's references into action. I was anxious to lie low, so applied here. The old woman considered herself lucky. So I got on without you, you see. You lie expecting me back, I don't come back.

You never considered yourself lucky. You considered you'd saddled yourself with a fool but you had to have me, I

81

was a fool to love you that way, you were quite right. We are quit of each other, if that was what you wanted you got what you wanted, it was what I wanted, perhaps all the time we were wanting the same thing, and now I've got that I don't want anything more. You thought I had to have you, as much as you thought you thought that. You thought that when you said what you said then, and you thought that under the pillow. When I took the pillow off that was in your eyes. Well, unthink that. If I thought you thought that still, if I thought you lay thinking that where you are now, I'd break right through, I'd tear anything down to get at you and tear the thought out, I'd tear up the sunk earth. Yes, it makes me mad to see you don't see that I don't see you or want you, that you don't see when these stairs creak outside that I don't think 'Here she is,' that I lie as still as you lie with my bed not creaking any more than your sunk earth and don't think, 'She was here once.' If I were to write, '*I love you, I cannot bear this, I want you, come back*' — you might be tricked. You might come back to see me see you, then you would see me not see you, you would unthink the thought you thought under the pillow, as much as you thought. Yes, look, if I tricked you this way, you'd come back, you could not not come back, you could never resist that. Yes, so look, I'll trick you I'll write loud, like a scream would be if anyone was in the dark with nothing (but I am not in the dark) I'll write so loud you will hear though you can't hear, *Anita*——

The pen charged in his hand. Dragging his hand down to the foot of the paper, in staggering charging characters it wrote — '*Anita, I love you Anita, Anita, where are you? I didn't mean that, that was not me, I didn't, I can't bear you away. I see your eyes on my pillow, I can't lie alone, I cannot get through the night, come back, where are you, I won't hurt you, come back, come back, come back——'*

Prothero dropped the pen as though it were burning. He watched it, frightfully animate, roll to the edge of the table and over the edge. He stared at his right hand and spread out the fingers slowly; they reasserted his will. Shutting his eyes, he screwed round full to the light of the four candles a blank-lidded square fair face clammy with sweat. His hands meanwhile groped over the table, gathering up by feel the close-written sheets. Rising, an automatic and mindless movement, he flung open the lid of the stove with a pothook and thrust the papers in, heard for a minute the hot red roar of the stove, then dropped the lid on the roar.

So his nights succeeded each other. At the back of the Manor House, through the ilex, a light was still burning in Mrs. Archworth's room. Downstairs, behind the red kitchen blind, a sleepy, indignant maid sat up for Davina. The village clock struck midnight with rolling strokes.

The wreathed gilt clock above Marianne's head struck midnight with brittle chimes, at which the air quivered like something stretched too tight. The chandelier glittering high up exhausted itself on the smoke, light losing quality as the evening wore on, and a sluggish chill crept over the party's wearied over-acute senses like a miasma. With drifts of cigarette ash in the lap of her black velvet skirt, Miriam sat talking introspectively to nobody in particular; she did not drink any more. The Russian played cat's cradle with a bit of gold cord from a chocolate-box. Purdon sat on a highish chair with his legs crossed, yawning at the chandelier. Mrs. Bennington slept on.

'You see, I'm that way,' went on Miriam. 'I don't believe in anything. I don't believe anything really exists, you see.'

The Russian slipped the gold cord off the tips of his fingers and, frowning with concentration, started over again. 'But look here,' said Purdon, 'if you're not going to believe in anything, you have to have something not to believe *in*.'

'*I* don't have to,' said Miriam. 'I can believe in nothing. I always could; I was always funny that way.'

'Do you believe in progress?' said the Russian.

'Everything's talk,' said Miriam, 'and what does all that come to? I see through it.'

'I don't, either,' said the Russian.

'And look at all this fuss all the time. Every time you pick up a paper there's a fuss about something. What I want to know is, what are they getting at? Have you any idea?' she said to Davina.

'No,' said Davina.

'I daresay you've never thought; I daresay you're right, too. What do *you* do?'

'Nothing,' replied Davina. 'I can't.'

'Oh, well,' said Miriam kindly, 'perhaps you've got money?'

'No, not now.'

'Dear me,' said Miriam, 'none of us have any luck. If you'd had a hundred pounds I'd have taken you into partnership. I'm looking round for a partner. Or, strictly, I'm looking round for a hundred pounds, but I wouldn't mind a partner; it would be company. Have you heard about me?'

'No. What?'

'I keep a tea-and-cake parlour called The Cat and Kettle. If you like cakes it's all right, but it puts you off them. It's not far from here, at Warring — on the river, you know. I've got check blinds and an inglenook and olde-oak beams and a cat; it's nice till you get used to it. I do Devonshire Teas at one and six and Dainty Teas *à la carte*. I lose on the Devonshires, mostly; you've no idea how much a person can eat to spite you. Still, it's a draw, and you've got to consider that. I wouldn't mind so much if it weren't for the black beetles; I always think they try and run up my legs. My cat eats them, but you should see how they multiply; however, don't tell me a cat's not faithful. I bake the stuff myself; I'm a real home girl, I am; there's plenty of use for a gas-oven without putting one's head in it, as I always tell the girls. Every now and then my hand goes right out; I don't mind telling you, you could knock a man down with some of my gingerbread. But people would eat a boot if it was home made. They like getting caraways into their teeth and spitting out burnt currants; it feels like the old home. I've had customers drive thirty miles to see the dear old black kettle sit on the hob and kid themselves I made the tea out of it. Neurotic, that's what they are. I get mostly courting couples; the girls like it; there's something about that kettle that brings a man to the point. He mashes my comb honey about and goes soppy about his mother; it makes you sick. You'd think it would make a girl sick, but a girl goes through worse than that, as I always say. However, no times like the old times—— Look in next time you're passing,' she said to Davina.

'I never am,' said Davina. 'I haven't got a car.'

'Well, you won't miss much,' said Miriam without rancour. 'It's a hole of a place where I am. Dishwater fogs all the winter and a slow motion High Street with no one about all day but the dear vicar. In summer it's like the inside of a hot pipe and you can't hear yourself think. Cars in a screaming jam all down the street, and punts jammed down the river till you couldn't drown a kitten between, and couples tie up all night, with ukuleles and portables, to the bank under my yard wall. You never know what goes on. It wouldn't be *your* cup of tea.'

'You know,' said Purdon to Miriam, 'you ought really to marry me.'

'Yes,' sighed the Russian, 'that's what I always say.' He put his head down on Mrs. Bennington's shoulder and dropped the twist of gold cord despondently into her lap.

All this time, Oliver had been standing above Marianne, leaning against the mantelpiece. He had said nothing since the clock struck, but now he turned and said eagerly to Marianne: 'Come for a turn.'

The fire had 'caught' and danced fluttering up, throwing pink light on the kerb: Marianne sat so close that a faint smell of wool scorching came from her skirt. She fixed her eyes on the smiling, familiar flames and felt more herself. Once or twice with a sleepy unconscious movement she leaned her forehead against the cold marble upright of the mantelpiece. Remotely she had heard midnight strike on the gilt clock. All the time she was aware with some apprehension of Oliver standing silently tall above her, like a tree that might fall. When he did speak, she looked away from him round the room with her frightened eyes: everything seemed to vacillate. The table toppling with bottles seemed to be balancing anxiously, splaying its gilt claw feet out on the parquet like an animal on the ice.

'Won't you come?' said Oliver.

'It's so late. It's so cold.'

'We will walk round the house.'

He opened the door; she rose and, unwinding her scarf from the Psyche, walked through the door ahead of him in a dream. The others said nothing. Like children in a large temple the two walked through the hall and up the bare white stone staircase, ascending to meet themselves in a darkish mirror at the head of the first flight. Here the staircase divided and rose in two sweeps like antlers against the high wall that was hung each side of the mirror with pastoral tapestries. From the head of each flight ran a gallery, waxy and dark. The house's great vacant height and resounding unlit perspectives weighed upon Marianne. As they went from room to room she heard Oliver's fingers tap in the dark on the wall for the light switch, then Italianate ceilings and sheeted icebergs of furniture sprang into cold existence. 'Think of living here!' she said.

'Where *do* you live?'

She began to explain. But she was held up by something ardent and curious in his manner, the impatience with which, shaking his lock of fair hair back, he stared through her outline, not seeming to listen. What she was saying trailed off into unimportance. Tonight and his presence tightened their hold on her spirit; the everyday became cloudy and meaningless and, like a tapestry, full of arrested movement. At the tapestry she looked down – for they had come back to the gallery. She stood fixing her eyes on the subfusc temples on hills and the nymphs trailing dead garlands, inanimate in brown gloom.

'Shan't I see you again, then?'

She did not know what to say.

'You tell me you're married,' Oliver said accusingly.

Coming in tonight with Davina, quite unexplained, she had seemed to him as disconnected from fact as an angel or goddess. Her lost face, mild wild air, and, once or twice as they groped through the dark house, her anxious touch on his arm, had set up in him a violent solicitude. Now, outraged by what she had only begun to tell him, he exclaimed excitedly: 'Damn the natural affections!'

'Oh, you mustn't say that!'

'They are a ramp,' said Oliver. One angry hand on her elbow, he wheeled her right about to face a pair of heavily moulded doors. He flung one of these open on a resounding void, announcing: 'The grand saloon.' They went in. He flicked at a half-dozen switches but no light came. 'The bulbs are all gone; he's as poor as a rat,' said Oliver.

Reflections from outside touched the glass fronts of cabinets; a white path of canvas drugget led off into the dark. The room sounded enormous. He pulled the sheet from a sofa and they sat down; behind them the door swung to with a heavy click and Marianne caught a breath. Oliver swooped on her two hands in the dark and kissed the side of her cheek as she leaned wildly away.

'This isn't the way to behave—'

'It's how I behave!' he said with a touch of hysteria.

'I'd rather go home.'

'I've been missing you all my life!'

'We can't meet again now!'

'For God's sake don't play-act!' said he.

Excitement with Oliver took its most crippling form. Her wrists encircled in his tyrannic clutch, Marianne heard his hurried breathing check and gather into a sob. A tear, then another, splashed on the back of her hand. Speechless, he let go her hands to dash the tears from his face. In the large unknown room a ring of autumnal silence, sealike and desolate in its unbounded nature, bore in on Marianne their distance from everything fixed.

'What's the matter?' she said.

'You're the last straw.'

'Haven't you got any home?'

'Damn, damn,' said Oliver at a fresh burst of tears. Fumbling and trembling, she thrust her cambric handkerchief into his hand. She put her arm round him, his head slid on to her shoulder, the sofa shook with a sob and he swore again.

'Why do you keep saying that?'

'This is not how I feel,' he said angrily.

'What can I do?'

Davina and Paul, the Russian, left the restless ante-room a few minutes later; they went for a turn, too, and wandered about the mansion, upstairs and down, knocking ash off their cigarettes. It was very cold; Davina stopped in the hall to put on her overcoat. They could see from lights on upstairs that the other two must be somewhere, and were uncertain whether to join them or not. They opened and shut doors without much curiosity. They sat down on a chest in the gallery, and Paul said how much mistaken Miriam was, not marrying Purdon, not believing in anything. Then he said he thought the end of the world would soon come.

'No doubt it's high time,' said Davina. 'But don't let's talk of it.'

'Who is your friend?'

'Marianne? She has a dull life. But look here, Paul: about me — I never know what to do.'

'Wait for something to happen.'

'I hate having no power. Tonight, for instance, I'm furious with someone.'

Not understanding, he looked at her sympathetically, got up and opened one of the grand saloon doors. They stood on the threshold and stared in at the dark. He said: 'The lights are not working.'

'Never mind, it's only a room.' They both turned away.

'All the same, we ought to find Oliver. It's high time Mrs. Bennington went to bed.'

Next morning, pale milky sunshine flooded the façade of Lord Thingummy's house. In a bedroom behind the parapet Mrs. Bennington, fully dressed under the eiderdown, lay breathing spirituously. The solitary housemaid, having risen at nine, opened the shutters all over the house, and long shafts of misty sunshine slid through the rooms. Patiently stooping, she picked up the cigarette-ends stamped out on the floors. In the grand saloon she sheeted up again an unsheeted sofa and picked up a lady's handkerchief and a striped woollen scarf. Downstairs, in the ante-room, the gilt clock had stopped at ten minutes to four: the hearth was white with cold wood-ash. The housemaid flung up a window and let out on to the morning the stale, cold fumes that hung like lead in the air. She sniffed each of the bottles and swept up some broken glass: a cigarette had burnt out in the trough of a brocade cushion. Fine dust lay everywhere; the sleepy housemaid bumped vaguely round with her broom, swirling the dust up and letting it settle again.

The housemaid's steps in the hollow house, her violence with the shutters and the knock of her broom, woke Oliver up. He woke saying 'She's gone,' and lay sprawled rigidly sideways across his bed with his eyes shut, unwilling to wake, while thoughts of his own ignobility raced through his brain ... The grass of the park rolled fawn-pale to the horizon in the veiled sunshine; the lake stretched bright white against a brown belt of trees, fringed with papery pale windless reeds. A swan slowly turned on the lake and a man on horseback rode along the bare skyline: nothing else moved. The outdoor world lay reflected in the dark glass of Oliver's mind as he lay, with his eyes shut, sideways across his bed; he groaned at the still morning scene as though he stood at his window. For himself he could see no reason. He had, unwillingly, deluded her with his tears: one cannot weep all the time. He longed to see himself otherwise, like any other man, with a sound and passionate core. He thought of the grand saloon with alarm and pity, as though she lay dead in there. Opening his eyes a moment on the accusing daylight, he rolled over to reach for his first cigarette . . . He never finished Lord Thingummy's catalogue.

A thin veil of river-mist lay on the Archworth garden. Davina woke late, looked at the unclear trees, and thought: 'At least we are honest.' Getting up, she found she had circles under her eyes: one did not grow any younger. She thought with relief of last night's pleasure, because it was over, because it had been so slight. She and her friends had come to the same sad age when one can change no longer, and only become more oneself. They could enthrall and bluff each other no longer — but still, to meet is to meet. They had made some kind of a hearth, and its warmth remained. Oliver with his dispirited Viking air, at once gallant and craven, and Paul with his placid and disenchanted smile, were renewed in her heart; she pictured Miriam on her high heels stepping over the beetles this morning and Purdon re-opening his surgery with a sigh. Combing back her springy dark hair and making up her mouth with pome-granate lipstick — alas! for no one — Davina thought of them kindly, regretting their premature autumn. 'We are not so bad,' she thought.

She went to her aunt's room.

Mrs. Archworth sat propped up in bed in a hug-me-tight trimmed with marabout. Beside the hot bedroom fire the Pekinese snored and dribbled. As Davina tapped on the door and came in smartly, resentment fought with affection on her aunt's face: 'I was a little anxious——' Mrs. Archworth began.

'But just you wait till you hear——'

Mrs. Archworth could not resist that flashing dark look. Poor plain pompous fussy old woman, no one else was at pains to fascinate her these days. She shifted her feet in bed, making room for Davina to sit, and patted the eiderdown with an uncertain smile. Davina explained with more than usual vividness how, Marianne's car having broken down, on a drive after dinner, outside unknown gates, the two had been for some hours the guests of Lord Thingummy.

'He would be kindness itself,' said her aunt. 'I once danced with him. And we dined there once, I remember, not long after your uncle and I were married. I am glad you should be making friends in the neighbourhood. This house, Davina, I'd like you to understand, is to be yours when I die.'

Davina said, startled: 'That's very good of you.'

Her aunt, with a wry and oddly dignified smile, said: 'My dear, I shall not need it.'

Marianne drove to meet Matthew at the 12.33 from London. The down platform was crowded, and for a moment or two of uncertain feeling she thought he had missed the train. Then he came ambling her way with light on his spectacles. His overcoat flapped and he carried a small dispatch-case. 'How is my girl?' he said, as they made their way through the barrier.

She was disorientated; she did not know. At home, she had not renewed the water in the bowls of chrysanthemums; it was a greenish colour, and stank faintly. The dogs, not yet exercised, fawned rather pointedly on the returning pair. The cat ran to meet them with its tail straight up; turned for no reason and ran away again. Mild unclear morning light filled the new white house with its evenly heated rooms. Matthew Harvey never kissed in a station, so half-way across the hall he put down his dispatch-case, closed the door to the kitchen, and kissed his wife. Colour rushed up her face, but he did not see.

He returned a book to the shelf and looked through a pile of letters. Meanwhile Marianne's look trailed wearily round the living-room, as though it were she who were just back from a journey and could still find no place to rest.

'I think,' said Matthew, 'I must get my glasses changed.'

'Changed?' said Marianne, starting.

'My glasses, yes,' said Matthew, leaning back in his chair and looking at her with affection. Then he stooped to pick up an end of white cotton from a hand-woven rug. He rolled this into a cocoon and flicked it into the fire. 'A bit of white cotton,' he said, 'but I picked it up.'

She stood with her back to him, looking out of the window, and said: 'The weathercock's pointing the other way.'

'The wind must have changed,' he said pleasantly.

She looked downhill, over the raw garden terraces, at the tops of the village trees with, in their heart, the glinting veering gold bird. Over the Archworths' chimneys a whorl of white smoke immobilized. Far off, across the flat water-meadows, the creeping red streets waited: beyond, a crowd of pale spires pricked the stooping grey sky. The world reflected itself in the vacant glass of her mind. Her hands, on which tears had fallen, vaguely clenched and unclenched in the pockets of her tweed coat.

'It is good to be back,' observed Matthew.

She did not reply.

'What's the matter?' he said. 'You're not quite yourself.'

'Perhaps I have got a slight chill.'

Davina looked over the net blind of Mrs. Archworth's window, down into the yard. There was no one about in the yard, least of all Prothero. Biting her lip, she stared down at the white cobbles, the cement incline to the garage, the drifted leaves. A flush of angry intention appeared on her cheekbones. 'What's that?' exclaimed Mrs. Archworth, struck by her rigid attitude. But the bedroom door had shut sharply: Davina was gone.

Inside its kennel, the foolish yard dog stirred with a rustle, dragging its chain in the straw; the pigeons rose wheeling on noisy wings. Davina slid back the garage door on its rollers, but found only the Daimler's wide polished back. The cook looked out of the back door and said that if it was Prothero anyone wanted, he had gone out.

'Why should he do that?'

'I couldn't tell you, I'm sure, miss. We're so independent, we are.'

Davina swung round and went out through the yard gate, down the lane to the village. Her tremendous anger made the village spread round the green, with its porches, dark little shop-fronts and stooping gables, look like a stage scene, a scene set for today. The raggy grass of the green was shredded with dead lime leaves, a smell of wood-smoke hung in the still air. Her look darted round the green; she had only one thought: 'He's gone.' That thought was bitter.

But Prothero came out of the grocer's opposite, with a felt hat pulled down over his forehead and a packet of candles under his arm. He stood in the shop door, not seeing Davina. Then, with his swinging, leisurely, damned independent stride, he started back round the green to the house again. Davina cut back before him to the mouth of the lane. She waited; they came face to face and Prothero pulled up patiently.

'Well?' said he.

'What about that message?'

'What about that money?'

'That's no way to talk — whoever you are.'

'It was good enough for you last night — whoever I am.'

94

She said contemptuously: 'I was in a hurry.'

'Oh, come,' said he, 'we had quite a pleasant chat.'

His light eyes and her dark eyes met implacably. Davina, driving her hands down into her pockets, said: 'They gave you a message for me. What became of it?'

'If your friends want to leave messages, they should go to the front door, not hang round the yard like tinkers. I'm not here to take messages; I am a busy man.'

'You'll be dismissed for this. You forget yourself.'

'I should like to,' he said, smiling without pleasure. 'But what would your aunt say to our little bill? I wouldn't upset her now you've feathered your nest so nicely. Besides, we should miss each other, I daresay.'

'That's blackmail,' she said. 'You're a crook, aren't you?'

'I got even with someone.'

'That was grand,' she said bitterly.

'Yes, I'm right on top of the world.' He looked up at the weathercock.

'You must be mad,' she said, looking at him intently. 'Else why spoil my evening? Why make an enemy of me? Suppose I gave you away?'

'You wouldn't do that if you could. For one thing, you haven't the guts, and it wouldn't get you anywhere. Spoil your evening?' He looked at her incuriously. 'How you do set your hearts on things!'

'A monkey trick,' she said scornfully. 'Oh, you're a great man!'

'Mmn. I do what I want. And I take what I want, I don't hang about for it. I wonder it doesn't sicken a girl like you, hanging about here, waiting. You'd better get out. I'm through. Don't keep coming after my money; it's not my money you want. I know your sort. Well, I'm through with all that. I'm buying not selling, these days. You keep your place, Miss Archworth, and I'll keep mine. You can't have it both ways. Good day.'

Nodding, he walked away from her down the lane. She followed him, at a distance, through the yard gates. He was mad, in plain terms — her own. She watched him, with fascination, cross the yard to his staircase. It was true she had, in some strange fashion, fed her own pride by the hasty sale of her kisses, feeling set free of herself each time those anonymous lips without pleasure had claimed her own, or those unseeing abstract cold eyes lit on her face. She went to the archway and called up the hollow staircase: 'Who *are* you?'

'My own man,' he said, and shut his door vigorously. Flakes of plaster slid from the staircase wall, and the steps creaked into silence after his tread. Davina felt in her pocket but found no cigarette. She called: 'I'm going,' and turned back to the house.

In the drawing-room, she filled up her case from the cigarette-box put out last night for the admiral and the Indian Civilian. The parrakeet wobbled on its perch; upstairs, she heard her aunt beginning to move about; she leaned on the mantelpiece thinking about Prothero: free men do not boast ... She decided to walk up, now, at once, to the Harvey's, to tell Marianne she was going away, would be quite gone in a week. But Matthew would be at home.

Davina walked up the hill, but not to the Harveys; straight up between the ruts of the half-made road; then she struck out across the grass to the water-tower. Along the brambly sky-line she walked rapidly, clicking her finger against her thumb and thinking: 'If I had money. . . .'

She saw that events led nowhere, crisis was an illusion, and that passions of momentary violent reality were struck off like sparks from the spirit, only to die. One could precipitate nothing. One is empowered to live fully: occasion does not offer. The whole panorama of life seemed spread out under this hill: between the brambles, hitting an old tin can with her stick idly, Davina stood still to stare . . . Downhill from the tower the gentlemanly new houses reflected the autumn daylight in steel-framed windows. As the sky sharpened with clouds and over the landscape the morning darkened, the skyline spires went leaden, the gasometer and the far-off curve of the river took on a wary glint. An almost inaudible hum of wind rising began below in the trees.

Davina decided to throw off her dashing character and ask her aunt for the money to repay Prothero. Two men came uphill her way, stopped and debated: they were surveyors coming to peg out a new road.

MARIA

'WE have girls of our own, you see,' Mrs. Dosely said, smiling warmly.

That seemed to settle it. Maria's aunt Lady Rimlade relaxed at last in Mrs. Dosely's armchair, and, glancing round once more at the Rectory drawing-room's fluttery white curtains, alert-looking photographs, and silver cornets spuming out pink sweet-pea, consigned Maria to these pleasant influences.

'Then that will be delightful,' she said in that blandly conclusive tone in which she declared open so many bazaars. 'Thursday *next*, then, Mrs. Dosely, about tea-time?'

'That will be delightful.'

'It is *most* kind,' Lady Rimlade concluded.

Maria could not agree with them. She sat scowling under her hat-brim, tying her gloves into knots. Evidently, she thought, I *am* being paid for.

Maria thought a good deal about money; she had no patience with other people's affectations about it, for she enjoyed being a rich little girl. She was only sorry not to know how much they considered her worth; having been sent out to walk in the garden while her aunt had just a short chat, dear, with the Rector's wife. The first phase of the chat, about her own character, she had been able to follow perfectly as she wound her way in and out of some crescent-shaped lobelia beds under the drawing-room window. But just as the two voices changed — one going unconcerned, one very, very diffident — Mrs. Dosely approached the window and, with an air of immense unconsciousness, shut it. Maria was baulked.

Maria was at one of those comfortable schools where everything is attended to. She was (as she had just heard her Aunt Ena explaining to Mrs. Dosely) a motherless girl, sensitive, sometimes difficult, deeply reserved. At school they took all this, with her slight tendency to curvature and her dislike of all puddings, into loving consideration. She was having her character 'done' for her — later on, when she came out, would be time for her hair and complexion. In addition to this, she learnt swimming, dancing, some French, the more innocent aspects of history, and *noblesse oblige*. It was a really nice school. All the same, when Maria came home for the holidays they could not do enough to console her for being a motherless girl who had been sent away.

Then, late last summer term, with inconceivable selfishness, her Uncle Philip fell ill and, in fact, nearly died. Aunt Ena had written less often and very distractedly, and when Maria came home she was told, with complete disregard for her motherlessness, that her uncle and aunt would be starting at once for a cruise, and that she was 'to be arranged for'.

This was not so easy. All the relations and all the family friends (who declared when Sir Philip was ill they'd do anything in the world), wrote back their deep disappointment at being unable to have Maria just now, though there was nothing, had things been otherwise, that they would have enjoyed more. One to his farm in fact, said Mr. MacRobert, the Vicar, when he was consulted, another to his merchandise. Then he suggested his neighbours, a Mr. and Mrs. Dosely, of Malton Peele. He came over to preach in Lent; Lady Rimlade had met him; he seemed such a nice man, frank, cheerful and earnest. *She* was exceedingly motherly, everyone said, and sometimes took in Indian children to make ends meet. The Doselys would be suitable, Maria's aunt felt at once. When Maria raged, she drew down urbane pink eyelids and said she did wish Maria would not be rude. So she drove Maria and the two little griffons over the next afternoon to call upon Mrs. Dosely. If Mrs. Dosely really seemed sympathetic, she thought she might leave the two little dogs with her too.

'And Mrs. Dosely has girls of her own, she tells me,' said Lady Rimlade on the way home. 'I should not wonder if you made quite friends with them. I should not wonder if it was they who had done the flowers. I thought the flowers were done very nicely; I noticed them. Of course, I do not care myself for small silver vases like that, shaped like cornets, but I thought the effect in the Rectory drawing-room very cheerful and homelike.'

Maria took up the word skilfully. 'I suppose no one,' she said, 'who has not been in my position can be expected to realize what it feels like to have no home.'

'Oh, Maria darling. . . .'

'I can't tell you what I think of this place you're sending me to,' said Maria. 'I bounced on the bed in that attic they're giving me and it's like iron. I suppose you realize that rectories are always full of diseases? Of course, I shall make the best of it, Aunt Ena. I shouldn't like you to feel I'd complained. But of course you don't realize a bit, do you, what I may be exposed to? So often carelessness about a girl at my age just ruins her life.'

Aunt Ena said nothing; she settled herself a little further down in the rugs and lowered her eyelids as though a strong wind were blowing.

That evening, on her way down to shut up the chickens, Mrs. Dosely came upon Mr. Hammond, the curate, rolling the cricket-pitch in the Rectory field. He was indefatigable, and, though more High Church than they cared for, had outdoor tastes. He came in to meals with them regularly, 'as an arrangement', because his present landlady could not cook and a young man needs to be built up, and her girls were still so young that no one could possibly call Mrs. Dosely designing. So she felt she ought to tell him.

'We shall be one more now in the house,' she said, 'till the end of the holidays. Lady Rimlade's little niece Maria — about fifteen — is coming to us while her uncle and aunt are away.'

'Jolly,' said Mr. Hammond sombrely, hating girls.

'We *shall* be a party, shan't we?'

'The more the merrier, I daresay,' said Mr. Hammond. He was a tall young man with a jaw, rather saturnine; he never said much, but Mrs. Dosely expected family life was good for him. 'Let 'em all come,' said Mr. Hammond, and went on rolling. Mrs. Dosely, with a tin bowl under one arm and a basket hooked on the other, stood at the edge of the pitch and watched him.

'She seemed a dear little thing — not pretty, but such a serious little face, full of character. An only child, you see. I said to her when they were going away that I expected she and Dilly and Doris would soon be inseparable, and her face quite lit up. She has no mother; it seems so sad.'

'*I* never had a mother,' said Mr. Hammond, tugging the roller grimly.

'Oh, I do *know*. But for a young girl I do think it still sadder . . . I thought Lady Rimlade charming; so unaffected. I said to her that we all lived quite simply here, and that if Maria came we should treat her as one of ourselves, and she said that was just what Maria would love . . . In age, you see, Maria comes just between Dilly and Doris.'

She broke off; she couldn't help thinking how three years

hence Maria might well be having a coming-out dance. Then she imagined herself telling her friend Mrs. Brotherhood: 'It's terrible, I never seem to see anything of my girls nowadays. They seem always to be over at Lady Rimlade's.'

'We must make the poor child feel at home here,' she told Mr. Hammond brightly.

The Doselys were accustomed to making the best of Anglo-Indian children, so they continued to be optimistic about Maria. 'One must make allowance for character', had become the watchword of this warm-hearted household, through which passed a constant stream of curates with tendencies, servants with tempers, unrealized lady visitors, and yellow-faced children with no morale. Maria was forbearingly swamped by the family; she felt as though she were trying to box an eiderdown. Doris and Dilly had indelibly creased cheeks: they kept on smiling and smiling. Maria couldn't decide how best to be rude to them; they taxed her resourcefulness. She could not know Dilly had thought, 'Her face is like a sick monkey's,' or that Doris, who went to one of those sensible schools, decided as soon that a girl in a diamond bracelet was shocking bad form. Dilly had repented at once of her unkind thought (though she had not resisted noting it in her diary), and Doris had simply said: 'What a pretty bangle. Aren't you afraid of losing it?' Mr. Dosely thought Maria striking-looking (she had a pale, square-jawed little face, with a straight fringe cut above scowling brows), striking but disagreeable — here he gave a kind of cough in his thoughts and, leaning forward, asked Maria if she were a Girl Guide.

Maria said she hated the sight of Girl Guides, and Mr. Dosely laughed heartily and said that this was a pity, because, if so, she must hate the sight of Doris and Dilly. The supper-table rocked with merriment. Shivering in her red *crêpe* frock (it was a rainy August evening, the room was fireless, a

window stood open, and outside the trees streamed coldly),
Maria looked across at the unmoved Mr. Hammond, square-
faced, set and concentrated over his helping of macaroni
cheese. He was not amused. Maria had always thought curates
giggled; she despised curates because they giggled, but was
furious with Mr. Hammond for not giggling at all. She studied
him for some time, and, as he did not look up, at last said:
'Are you a Jesuit?'

Mr. Hammond (who had been thinking about the cricket
pitch) started violently; his ears went crimson; he sucked in
one last streamer of macaroni. 'No,' he said, 'I am not a
Jesuit. Why?'

'Oh, nothing,' said Maria. 'I just wondered. As a matter of
fact, I don't know what Jesuits are.'

Nobody felt quite comfortable. It was a most unfortunate
thing, in view of the nature of Mr. Hammond's tendencies,
for poor little Maria, in innocence, to have said. Mr. Hammond's tendencies were so marked, and, knowing how
marked the Doselys thought his tendencies were, he was
touchy. Mrs. Dosely said she expected Maria must be very
fond of dogs. Maria replied that she did not care for any dogs
but Alsatians. Mrs. Dosely was glad to be able to ask Mr.
Hammond if it were not he who had told her that he had a
cousin who bred Alsatians. Mr. Hammond said that this was
the case. 'But unfortunately,' he added, looking across at
Maria, 'I dislike Alsatians intensely.'

Maria now realized with gratification that she had incurred
the hatred of Mr. Hammond. This was not bad for one evening. She swished her plateful of macaroni round with her fork
then put the fork down pointedly. Undisguised wholesome-
ness was, in food as in personalities, repellent to Maria. 'This
is the last supper but three — no, but two,' she said to herself,
'that I shall eat at this Rectory.'

It had all seemed so simple, it seemed so simple still, yet five nights afterwards found her going to bed once again in what Mrs. Dosely called the little white nest that we keep for our girl friends. Really, if one came to look at it one way, the Doselys were an experience for Maria, who had never till now found anybody who could stand her when she didn't mean to be stood. French maids, governesses, highly paid, almost bribed into service, had melted away. There was something marvellously, memorably un-winning about Maria . . . Yet here she still was. She had written twice to her aunt that she couldn't sleep and couldn't eat here, and feared she must be unwell, and Lady Rimlade wrote back advising her to have a little talk about all this with Mrs. Dosely. Mrs. Dosely, Lady Rimlade pointed out, was motherly. Maria told Mrs. Dosely she was afraid she was unhappy and couldn't be well. Mrs. Dosely exclaimed at the pity this was, but at all costs — Maria would see? — Lady Rimlade must not be worried. She had so expressly asked not to be worried at all.

'And she's so *kind*,' said Mrs. Dosely, patting Maria's hand.

Maria simply thought, 'This woman is mad.' She said with a wan smile that she was sorry, but having her hand patted gave her pins and needles. But rudeness to Mrs. Dosely was like dropping a pat of butter on to a hot plate — it slid and melted away.

In fact, all this last week Maria's sole consolation had been Mr. Hammond. Her pleasure in Mr. Hammond was so intense that three days after her coming he told Mrs. Dosely he didn't think he'd come in for meals any more, thank you, as his landlady had by now learned to cook. Even so, Maria had managed to see quite a lot of him. She rode round the village after him, about ten yards behind, on Doris's bicycle; she was there when he offered a prayer with the Mothers' Union; she never forgot to come out when he was at work on the cricket-pitch ('Don't you seem to get rather hot?' she would ask him feelingly, as he mopped inside his collar. 'Or are you really not as hot as you seem?'), and, having discovered that at six every evening he tugged a bell, then read Evensong in the church to two ladies, she came in alone every evening and sat in the front pew, looking up at him. She led the responses, waiting courteously for Mr. Hammond when he lost his place.

But tonight Maria came briskly, mysteriously up to the little white nest, locking the door for fear Mrs. Dosely might come in to kiss her good night. She could now agree that music was inspiring. For they had taken her to the Choral Society's gala, and the effect it had had on Maria's ideas was stupendous. Half-way through a rondo called '*Off to the Hills*' it had occurred to her that when she got clear of the Rectory she would go off to Switzerland, stay in a Palace Hotel, and do a little climbing. She would take, she thought, a hospital nurse, in case she hurt herself climbing, and an Alsatian to bother the visitors in the hotel. She had glowed — but towards the end of '*Hey, nonny, nonny*' a finer and far more constructive idea came along, eclipsing the other. She clapped her handkerchief to her mouth and, conveying to watchful Dilly that she might easily be sick at any moment, quitted the schoolhouse hurriedly. Safe in her white nest, she put her candlestick down with a bump, got her notepaper out, and sweeping her hair-brushes off the dressing-table, sat down at it to write thus:

Dearest Aunt Ena: You must wonder why I have not written for so long. The fact is, all else has been swept from my mind by one great experience. I hardly know how to put it all into words. The fact is I love a Mr. Hammond, who is the curate here, and am loved by him, we are engaged really and hope to be married quite shortly. He is a fascinating man, extremely High Church, he has no money but I am quite content to live

with him as a poor man's wife as I shall have to do if you and
Uncle Philip are angry, though you may be sorry when I
bring my little children to your door to see you. If you do not
give your consent we shall elope but I am sure, dear Aunt Ena,
that you will sympathize with your little niece in her great
happiness. All I beseech is that you will not take me away
from the Rectory; I do not think I could live without seeing
Wilfred every day — or every night rather, as we meet in the
churchyard and sit on a grave with our arms round each other
in the moonlight. The Doselys do not know as I felt it was
my duty to tell you first, but I expect the village people may
have noticed as unfortunately there is a right of way through
the churchyard but we cannot think of anywhere else to sit.
Is it not curious to think how true it was when I said at the
time when you sent me to the Rectory, that you did not
realize what you might be exposing me to? But now I am so
thankful that you did expose me, as I have found my great
happiness here, and am so truly happy in a good man's love.
Goodbye, I must stop now as the moon has risen and I am
just going out to meet Wilfred.

Your loving, full-hearted little niece,   MARIA

Maria, pleased on the whole with this letter, copied it out
twice, addressed the neater copy with a flourish, and went to
bed. The muslin frills of the nest moved gently on the night
air; the moon rose beaming over the churchyard and the pale
evening primroses fringing the garden path. No daughter of
Mrs. Dosely's could have smiled more tenderly in the dark
or fallen asleep more innocently.

Mr. Hammond had no calendar in his rooms: he was sent
so many at Christmas that he threw them all away and was
left with none, so he ticked off the days mentally. Three

weeks and six long days had still to elapse before the end of
Maria's visit. He remained shut up in his rooms for mornings
together, to the neglect of the parish, and was supposed to be
writing a book on Cardinal Newman. Postcards of arch white
kittens stepping through rosy wreaths arrived for him daily;
once he had come in to find a cauliflower labelled. 'From an
admirer' on his sitting-room table. Mrs. Higgins, the landlady, said the admirer must have come in by the window, as
she had admitted no one, so recently Mr. Hammond lived
with his window hasped. This morning, the Saturday after
the Choral Society's gala, as he sat humped over his table
writing his sermon, a shadow blotted the lower window-panes.
Maria, obscuring what light there was in the room with her
body, could see in only with difficulty; her nose appeared
white and flattened; she rolled her eyes ferociously round the
gloom. Then she began trying to push the window up.

'*Go away!*' shouted Mr. Hammond, waving his arms
explosively, as at a cat.

'You must let me in, I have something awful to tell you,'
shouted Maria, lips close to the pane. He didn't, so she went
round to the front door and was admitted by Mrs. Higgins
with due ceremony. Mrs. Higgins, beaming, ushered in the
little lady from the Rectory who had come, she said, with an
urgent message from Mrs. Dosely.

Maria came in, her scarlet beret tipped up, with the jaunty
and gallant air of some young lady intriguing for Bonny
Prince Charlie.

'Are we alone?' she said loudly, then waited for Mrs.
Higgins to shut the door. 'I thought of writing to you,' she
continued, 'but your coldness to me lately led me to think that
was hopeless.' She hooked her heels on his fender and stood
rocking backwards and forwards. 'Mr. Hammond, I warn
you: you must leave Malton Peele at once.'

'I wish *you* would,' said Mr. Hammond, who, seated, looked past her left ear with a calm concentration of loathing.

'I daresay I may,' said Maria, 'but I don't want you to be involved in my downfall. You have your future to think of; you may be a bishop; I am only a woman. You see, the fact is, Mr. Hammond, from the way we have been going about together, many people think we must be engaged. I don't want to embarrass you, Mr. Hammond.'

Mr. Hammond was not embarrassed. 'I always have thought you a horrid little girl, but I never knew you were quite so silly,' he said.

'We've been indiscreet. I don't know what my uncle will say. I only hope you won't be compelled to marry me.'

'Get off that fender,' said Mr. Hammond; 'you're ruining it . . . Well then, stay there; I want to look at you. I must say you're something quite new.'

'Yes, aren't I?' said Maria complacently.

'Yes. Any other ugly, insignificant-looking little girls I've known did something to redeem themselves from absolute unattractiveness by being pleasant, say, or a little helpful, or sometimes they were well bred, or had good table manners, or were clever and amusing to talk to. If it were not for the consideration of the Doselys for your unfortunate aunt — who is, I understand from Mr. Dosely, so stupid as to be almost mentally deficient — they would keep you — since they really have guaranteed to keep you — in some kind of shed or loose-box at the bottom of the yard . . . I don't want to speak in anger,' went on Mr. Hammond, 'I hope I'm not angry; I'm simply sorry for you. I always knew the Doselys took in Anglo-Indian children, but if I'd known they dealt in . . . cases . . . of your sort, I doubt if I'd have ever come to Malton Peele—— Shut up, you little hell-cat! I'll teach you to pull my hair——'

She was on top of him all at once, tweaking his hair with science.

'You beastly Bolshevik!' exclaimed Maria, tugging. He caught her wrists and held them. 'Oh! Shut up — you hurt me, you beastly bully, you! Oh! how could you hurt a girl!' She kicked at his shin, weeping. 'I — I only came,' she said, 'because I was sorry for you. I needn't have come. And then you go and start beating me up like this——*Ow!*'

'It's your only hope,' said Mr. Hammond with a vehement, grave, but very detached expression, twisting her wrist round further. 'Yes, go on, yell — I'm not hurting you. You may be jolly thankful I *am* a curate . . . As a matter of fact, I got sacked from my prep school for bullying . . . Odd how these things come back. . . .'

They scuffled. Maria yelped sharply and bit his wrist. 'Ha, you would, would you? . . . Oh, yes, I know you're a little girl — and a jolly nasty one. The only reason I've ever seen why one wasn't supposed to knock little girls about is that they're generally supposed to be nicer — pleasanter — prettier — than little boys.' He parried a kick and held her at arm's length by her wrists. They glared at each other, both crimson with indignation.

'And you supposed to be a curate!'

'And you supposed to be a lady, you little parasite! This'll teach you—— Oh!' said Mr. Hammond, sighing luxuriously, 'how pleased the Doselys would be if they knew!'

'Big brute! You great hulking brute!'

'If you'd been my little sister,' said Mr. Hammond, regretful, 'this would have happened before. But by this time, of course, you wouldn't be nearly so nasty . . . I should chivvy you round the garden and send you up a tree every day.'

'*Socialist!*'

'Well, get along now.' Mr. Hammond let go of her wrists.

'You can't go out of the door with a face like that; if you don't want a crowd you'd better go through the window . . . Now you run home and snivel to Mrs. Dosely.'

'*This* will undo your career,' Maria said, nursing wrists balefully. 'I shall have it put in the papers: "*Baronet's niece tortured by demon curate.*" That will undo your career for you, Mr. Hammond.'

'I know, I *know*, but it's worth it!' Mr. Hammond exclaimed exaltedly. He was twenty-four, and intensely meant what he said. He pushed up the window. 'Now get out,' he stormed, 'or I'll certainly kick you through it.'

'You are in a kind of a way like a brother to me, aren't you? remarked Maria, lingering on the sill.

'I am not. Get out!'

'But oh, Mr. Hammond, I came here to make a confession. I didn't expect violence, as no one's attacked me before. But I forgive you because it was righteous anger. I'm afraid we *are* rather compromised. You must read this. I posted one just the same to Aunt Ena three days ago.'

Maria handed over the copy of her letter.

'I may be depraved and ugly and bad, but you must admit, Mr. Hammond, I'm not stupid.' She watched him read.

Half an hour later Mr. Hammond, like a set of walking fire-irons, with Maria, limp as a rag, approached the Rectory. Maria hiccupped and hiccupped; she'd found Mr. Hammond had no sense of humour at all. She was afraid he was full of vanity. 'You miserable little liar,' he'd said quite distantly, as though to a slug, and here she was being positively bundled along. If there'd been a scruff to her neck he would have grasped it. Maria had really enjoyed being bullied, but she did hate being despised. Now they were both going into the study to have yet another scene with Mr. and Mrs. Dosely.

She was billed, it appeared, for yet another confession, and she had been so much shaken about that her technique faltered and she couldn't think where to begin. She wondered in a dim way what was going to happen next, and whether Uncle Philip would be coming to find Mr. Hammond with a horse-whip.

Mr. Hammond was all jaw; he wore a really disagreeable expression. Doris Dosely, up in the drawing-room window, gazed with awe for a moment, then disappeared.

'Doris!' yelled Mr. Hammond. 'Where is your father? Maria has something to tell him.'

'Dunno,' said Doris, and reappeared in the door. 'But here's a telegram for Maria — mother has opened it: something about a letter.'

'It would be,' said Mr. Hammond. 'Give it me here.'

'I can't, I won't,' said Maria, backing away from the telegram. Mr. Hammond, gritting his teeth audibly, received the paper from Doris.

YOUR LETTER BLOWN FROM MY HAND OVERBOARD: [he read out], AFTER HAD READ FIRST SENTENCE WILD WITH ANXIETY PLEASE REPEAT CONTENTS BY TELEGRAM YOUR UNCLE PHILIP WISHES YOU JOIN US MARSEILLES WEDNESDAY AM WRITING DOSELYS AUNT ENA.

'How highly strung poor Lady Rimlade must be,' said Doris kindly.

'She is a better aunt than many people deserve,' said Mr. Hammond.

'I think I may feel dull on that dreary old cruise after the sisterly, brotherly family life I've had here,' said Maria wistfully.

HER TABLE SPREAD

A LBAN had few opinions on the subject of marriage; his attitude to women was negative, but in particular he was not attracted to Miss Cuffe. Coming down early for dinner, red satin dress cut low, she attacked the silence with loud laughter before he had spoken. He recollected having heard that she was abnormal — at twenty-five, of statuesque development, still detained in childhood. The two other ladies, in beaded satins, made entrances of a surprising formality. It occurred to him, his presence must constitute an occasion: they certainly sparkled. Old Mr. Rossiter, uncle to Mrs. Treye, came last, more sourly. They sat for some time without the addition of lamplight. Dinner was not announced; the ladies by remaining on guard, seemed to deprecate any question of its appearance. No sound came from other parts of the Castle.

Miss Cuffe was an heiress to whom the Castle belonged and whose guests they all were. But she carefully followed the movements of her aunt, Mrs. Treye; her ox-eyes moved from face to face in happy submission rather than expectancy. She was continually preoccupied with attempts at gravity, as though holding down her skirts in a high wind. Mrs. Treye and Miss Carbin combined to cover her excitement; still, their looks frequently stole from the company to the windows, of which there were too many. He received a strong impression someone outside was waiting to come in. At last, with a sigh they got up: dinner had been announced.

The Castle was built on high ground, commanding the estuary; a steep hill, with trees, continued above it. On fine days the view was remarkable, of almost Italian brilliance, with that constant reflection up from the water that even now prolonged the too-long day. Now, in continuous evening rain, the winding wooded line of the further shore could be seen and, nearer the windows, a smothered island with the stump of a watch-tower. Where the Castle stood, a higher tower had answered the island's. Later a keep, then wings, had been added; now the fine peaceful residence had French windows opening on to the terrace. Invasions from the water would henceforth be social, perhaps amorous. On the slope down from the terrace, trees began again; almost, but not quite concealing the destroyer. Alban, who knew nothing, had not yet looked down.

It was Mr. Rossiter who first spoke of the destroyer — Alban meanwhile glancing along the table; the preparations had been stupendous. The destroyer had come today. The ladies all turned to Alban: the beads on their bosoms sparkled. So this was what they had here, under their trees. Engulfed by their pleasure, from now on he disappeared personally. Mr. Rossiter, rising a note, continued. The estuary, it appeared, was deep, with a channel buoyed up it. By a term of the Treaty, English ships were permitted to anchor in these waters.

'But they've been afraid of the rain!' chimed in Valeria Cuffe.

'Hush,' said her aunt, 'that's silly. Sailors would be accustomed to getting wet.'

But, Miss Carbin reported, that spring there *had* already been one destroyer. Two of the officers had been seen dancing at the hotel at the head of the estuary.

'So,' said Alban, 'you are quite in the world.' He adjusted his glasses in her direction.

Miss Carbin — blonde, not forty, and an attachment of Mrs. Treye's — shook her head despondently. 'We were all away at Easter. Wasn't it curious they should have come then? The sailors walked in the demesne but never touched the daffodils.'

'As though I should have cared!' exclaimed Valeria passionately.

'Morale too good,' stated Mr. Rossiter.

'But next evening,' continued Miss Carbin, 'the officers did not go to the hotel. They climbed up here through the trees to the terrace — you see, they had no idea. Friends of ours were staying here at the Castle, and they apologized. Our friends invited them in to supper. . . .'

'Did they accept?'

The three ladies said in a breath: 'Yes, they came.'

Valeria added urgently, 'So don't you *think*——?'

'So tonight we have a destroyer to greet you,' Mrs. Treye said quickly to Alban. 'It is quite an event; the country people are coming down from the mountains. These waters are very lonely; the steamers have given up since the bad times; there is hardly a pleasure-boat. The weather this year has driven visitors right away.'

'You are beautifully remote.'

'Yes,' agreed Miss Carbin. 'Do you know much about the Navy? Do you think, for instance, that this is likely to be the same destroyer?'

'*Will they remember?*' Valeria's bust was almost on the table. But with a rustle Mrs. Treye pressed Valeria's toe. For the dining-room also looked out across the estuary, and the great girl had not once taken her eyes from the window. Perhaps it was unfortunate that Mr. Alban should have coincided with the destroyer. Perhaps it was unfortunate for Mr. Alban too.

For he saw now he was less than half the feast; unappeased, the party sat looking through him, all grouped at an end of the table — to the other, chairs had been pulled up. Dinner was being served very slowly. Candles — possible to see from the water — were lit now; some wet peonies glistened. Outside, day still lingered hopefully. The bushes over the edge of the terrace were like heads — you could have sworn sometimes you saw them mounting, swaying in manly talk. Once, wound up in the rain, a bird whistled, seeming hardly a bird.

'Perhaps since then they have been to Greece, or Malta?'

'That would be the Mediterranean fleet,' said Mr. Rossiter.

They were sorry to think of anything out in the rain to-night.

'The decks must be streaming,' said Miss Carbin.

Then Valeria, exclaiming, 'Please excuse me!' pushed her chair in and ran from the room.

'She is impulsive,' explained Mrs. Treye. 'Have *you* been to Malta, Mr. Alban?'

In the drawing-room, empty of Valeria, the standard lamps had been lit. Through their ballet-skirt shades, rose and lemon, they gave out a deep, welcoming light. Alban, at the ladies' invitation, undraped the piano. He played, but they could see he was not pleased. It was obvious he had always been a civilian, and when he had taken his place on the piano-stool — which he twirled round three times, rather fussily — his dinner-jacket wrinkled across the shoulders. It was sad they should feel so indifferent, for he came from London. Mendelssohn was exasperating to them — they opened all four windows to let the music downhill. They preferred not to draw the curtains; the air, though damp, being pleasant tonight, they said.

The piano was damp, but Alban played almost all his heart out. He played out the indignation of years his mild manner concealed. He had failed to love; nobody did anything about this; partners at dinner gave him less than half their attention.

116

He knew some spring had dried up at the root of the world. He was fixed in the dark rain, by an indifferent shore. He played badly, but they were unmusical. Old Mr. Rossiter, who was not what he seemed, went back to the dining-room to talk to the parlourmaid.

Valeria, glittering vastly, appeared in a window.

'Come *in*!' her aunt cried in indignation. She would die of a chill, childless, in fact unwedded; the Castle would have to be sold and where would they all be?

But — 'Lights down there!' Valeria shouted above the music.

They had to run out for a moment, laughing and holding cushions over their bare shoulders. Alban left the piano; they looked boldly down from the terrace. Indeed, there they were: two lights like arc-lamps, blurred by rain and drawn down deep in reflection into the steady water. There were, too, ever so many portholes, all lit up.

'Perhaps they are playing bridge,' said Miss Carbin.

'Now I wonder if Uncle Robert ought to have called,' said Mrs. Treye. 'Perhaps we have seemed remiss — one calls on a regiment.'

'Patrick could row him out tomorrow.'

'He hates the water.' She sighed. 'Perhaps they will be gone.'

'Let's go for a row now — let's go for a row with a lantern,' besought Valeria, jumping and pulling her aunt's elbow. They produced such indignation she disappeared again — wet satin skirts and all — into the bushes. The ladies could do no more: Alban suggested the rain might spot their dresses.

'They must lose a great deal, playing cards throughout an evening for high stakes,' Miss Carbin said with concern as they all sat down again.

'Yet, if you come to think of it, somebody must win.'

But the naval officers who so joyfully supped at Easter had

been, Miss Carbin knew, a Mr. Graves, and a Mr. Garrett: *they* would certainly lose. 'At all events, it is better than dancing at the hotel; there would be nobody of their type.'

'There is nobody there at all.'

'I expect they are best where they are ... Mr. Alban, a Viennese waltz?'

He played while the ladies whispered, waving the waltz time a little distractedly. Mr. Rossiter, coming back, momentously stood: they turned in hope: even the waltz halted. But he brought no news. 'You should call Valeria in. You can't tell who may be round the place. She's not fit to be out tonight.'

'Perhaps she's not out.'

'She is,' said Mr. Rossiter crossly. 'I just saw her racing past the window with a lantern.'

Valeria's mind was made up: she was a princess. Not for nothing had she had the dining-room silver polished and all set out. She would pace around in red satin that swished behind, while Mr. Alban kept on playing a loud waltz. They would be dazed at all she had to offer — also her two new statues and the leopard-skin from the auction.

When he and she were married (she inclined a little to Mr. Garrett) they would invite all the Navy up the estuary and give them tea. Her estuary would be filled up, like a regatta, with loud excited battleships tooting to one another and flags flying. The terrace would be covered with grateful sailors, leaving room for the band. She would keep the peacocks her aunt did not allow. His friends would be surprised to notice that Mr. Garrett had meanwhile become an admiral, all gold. He would lead the other admirals into the castle and say, while they wiped their feet respectfully: 'These are my wife's statues; she has given them to me. One is Mars, one is Mercury. We have a Venus, but she is not dressed. And wait till I show you our silver and gold plates . . .' The Navy would be unable to tear itself away.

She had been excited for some weeks at the idea of marrying Mr. Alban, but now the lovely appearance of the destroyer put him out of her mind. He would not have done; he was not handsome. But she could keep him to play the piano on quiet afternoons.

Her friends had told her Mr. Garrett was quite a Viking. She was so very familiar with his appearance that she felt some-times they had already been married for years — though still, sometimes, he could not realize his good luck. She still had to remind him the island was hers too . . . Tonight, Aunt and darling Miss Carbin had so fallen in with her plans, putting on their satins and decorating the drawing-room, that the dinner became a betrothal feast. There was some little hitch about the arrival of Mr. Garrett — she had heard that gentle-men sometimes could not tie their ties. And now he was late and would be discouraged. So she must now go half-way down to the water and wave a lantern.

But she put her two hands over the lantern, then smothered it in her dress. She had a panic. Supposing she should prefer Mr. Graves?

She had heard Mr. Graves was stocky, but very merry; when he came to supper at Easter he slid in the gallery. He would teach her to dance, and take her to Naples and Paris. . . . Oh, dear, oh, dear, then they must fight for her; that was all there was to it . . . She let the lantern out of her skirts and waved. Her fine arm with bangles went up and down, up and down, with the staggering light; the trees one by one jumped up from the dark, like savages.

Inconceivably, the destroyer took no notice.

Undisturbed by oars, the rain stood up from the water; not

a light rose to peer, and the gramophone, though it remained very faint, did not cease or alter.

In mackintoshes, Mr. Rossiter and Alban meanwhile made their way to the boat-house, Alban did not know why. 'If that goes on,' said Mr. Rossiter, nodding towards Valeria's lantern, 'they'll fire one of their guns at us.'

'Oh, no. Why?' said Alban. He buttoned up, however, the collar of his mackintosh.

'Nervous as cats. It's high time that girl was married. She's a nice girl in many ways, too.'

'Couldn't we get the lantern away from her?' They stepped on a paved causeway and heard the water nibble the rocks.

'She'd scream the place down. She's of age now, you see.'

'But if——'

'Oh, she won't do that; I was having a bit of fun with you.' Chuckling equably, Mrs. Treye's uncle unlocked and pulled open the boat-house door. A bat whistled out.

'Why are we here?'

'She might come for the boat; she's a fine oar,' said Mr. Rossiter wisely. The place was familiar to him; he lit an oil-lamp and, sitting down on a trestle with a staunch air of having done what he could, reached a bottle of whisky out of the boat. He motioned the bottle to Alban. 'It's a wild night,' he said. 'Ah, well, we don't have these destroyers every day.'

'That seems fortunate.'

'Well, it is and it isn't.' Restoring the bottle to the vertical, Mr. Rossiter continued: 'It's a pity you don't want a wife. You'd be the better for a wife, d'you see, a young fellow like you. She's got a nice character; she's a girl you could shape. She's got a nice income.' The bat returned from the rain and knocked round the lamp. Lowering the bottle frequently, Mr. Rossiter talked to Alban (whose attitude remained negative) of women in general and the parlourmaid in particular. . . .

'*Bat!*' Alban squealed irrepressibly, and with his hand to his ear — where he still felt it — fled from the boat-house. Mr. Rossiter's conversation continued. Alban's pumps squelched as he ran; he skidded along the causeway and baulked at the upward steps. His soul squelched equally: he had been warned, he had been warned. He had heard they were all mad; he had erred out of headiness and curiosity. A degree of terror was agreeable to his vanity: by express wish he had occupied haunted rooms. Now he had no other pumps in this country, no idea where to buy them, and a ducal visit ahead. Also, wandering as it were among the apples and amphoras of an art school, he had blundered into the life room: woman revolved gravely.

'Hell,' he said to the steps, mounting, his mind blank to the outcome.

He was nerved for the jumping lantern, but half-way up to the Castle darkness was once more absolute. Her lantern had gone out; he could orientate himself — in spite of himself — by her sobbing. Absolute desperation. He pulled up so short that, for balance, he had to cling to a creaking tree.

'Hi!' she croaked. Then: 'You *are* there! I hear you!'

'Miss Cuffe——'

'How too bad you are! I never heard you rowing. I thought you were never coming——'

'Quietly, my dear girl.'

'Come up quickly. I haven't even seen you. Come up to the windows——'

'Miss Cuffe——'

'Don't you remember the way?' As sure but not so noiseless as a cat in the dark, Valeria hurried to him.

'Mr. Garrett——' she panted. 'I'm Miss Cuffe. Where have you been? I've destroyed my beautiful red dress and they've eaten up your dinner. But we're still waiting. Don't be afraid; you'll soon be there now. I'm Miss Cuffe; this is my Castle——'

'Listen, it's I, Mr. Alban——.

'Ssh, ssh, Mr. Alban: *Mr. Garrett has landed.*'

Her cry, his voice, some breath of the joyful intelligence, brought the others on to the terrace, blind with lamplight.

'Valeria?'

'Mr. Garrett has landed!'

Mrs. Treye said to Miss Carbin under her breath, 'Mr. Garrett has come.'

Miss Carbin, half weeping with agitation, replied, 'We must go in.' But uncertain who was to speak next, or how to speak, they remained leaning over the darkness. Behind, through the windows, lamps spread great skirts of light, and Mars and Mercury, unable to contain themselves, stooped from their pedestals. The dumb keyboard shone like a ballroom floor.

Alban, looking up, saw their arms and shoulders under the bright rain. Close by, Valeria's fingers creaked on her warm wet satin. She laughed like a princess, magnificently justified. Their unseen faces were all three lovely, and, in the silence after the laughter, such a strong tenderness reached him that, standing there in full manhood, he was for a moment not exiled. For the moment, without moving or speaking, he stood, in the dark, in a flame, as though all three said: 'My darling. . . .'

Perhaps it was best for them all that early, when next day first lightened the rain, the destroyer steamed out — below the extinguished Castle where Valeria lay with her arms wide, past the boat-house where Mr. Rossiter lay insensible and the bat hung masked in its wings — down the estuary into the open sea.

THE LITTLE GIRL'S ROOM

THIS was Geraldine's moment. At a nod from Mrs. Letherton-Channing, carefully guarding the flame of her taper, she passed round the circle from cigarette to cigarette. The little girl's serious movements, the pretty shell of her hand, the soft braids of hair as she stooped, swinging over her shoulders, the soft creak of her plaited sandals as she stepped, cast some kind of spell on the talk: silence followed her like a shadow.

At first Clara Ellis frowned: talk of a first-rate scandalous quality had been held up. But: 'Why,' she exclaimed, glancing at Geraldine's arm, 'you freckle just like a cowslip!'

'Do I?' blushed Geraldine.

They all said 'Dear thing' ... or 'How good of you, Geraldine dear.'

General Littlecote ducked to the flame in her hands rather grimly, as though the pleasure were bitter. Smoke began to go up in the afternoon light of the room; the green-panelled drawing-room, with bowls of lush yellow roses, ornate with Florentine furniture: smoke wreathed out of the high open windows across the magnolia flowering unseen. Geraldine reached her step-grandmother's chair and politely waited.

'Mr. Scutcheon is late,' said Mrs. Letherton-Channing.

'He's come,' said Geraldine gently. 'I saw him come up through the garden.'

'Really,' exclaimed Mrs. Letherton-Channing. 'How should he know the way?' Her face became expressionless with annoyance. For who knew how this might end? Indeed, it would never do to have professors of Greek and Latin, Italian and German masters, mathematicians, historians and even Swedish exponents of physical culture, finding their way through her garden at every hour. Meditation and intimate talk became imperilled. For Geraldine was being highly educated at home.

'Perhaps Miss Weekes showed him,' said Geraldine. 'Ought I to go?' she added.

'Why, certainly, if he *is* here,' snapped Mrs. Letherton-Channing. Her friends all realized that Mr. Scutcheon had come too soon.

Mrs. Letherton-Channing was a widow, with one step-son. The son's wife, Vivien, a difficult and rather derisive step-daughter-in-law, having died four years ago, the elder Mrs. Letherton-Channing thereby succeeded to what she was determined to prove a wonder-child. Vivien had once kept her Geraldine very much to herself, but nowadays Mrs. Letherton-Channing, in the strong position of being alive, could speak generously of her daughter-in-law, for Luke Letherton-Channing, distracted and set on flight to the ends of the earth, had, on his wife's death, immediately brought the eight-year-old to his step-mother's Italianate house in Berkshire.

Here Vivien, to whom such a question now became immaterial, had once declared that she could never breathe. 'Take Geraldine there?' she exclaimed. 'Why, she'd turn into a horrible little Verrocchio over a fountain!' But Vivien, whose departure from life had been despairing and hurried, had not tried to exact from Luke a promise he could not stand by. She died leaving bills unpaid, invitations unanswered, no word as to her child's future.

So the child came to Mrs. Letherton-Channing's house, where one had the impression of dignified exile, where British integrity seemed to have camped on a Tuscan hill, where

English midsummer did not exceed Italian April — roses wearing into July an air of delicate pre-maturity — and high noon reflected upon the ceilings a sheen of ilex and olive. Here the very guests seemed expatriate, and coal-fires, ruddy ghosts of themselves, roared under mantles crusted and swagged with glazed Della Robbia lemons and bluish pears. Clara Ellis, who was at least sincerely malicious, professed to adore this little Italy from Wigmore Street. From any window, she said, the strong eye of faith could ride a Gozzoli distance while an English February sleeted or robins starved in the frost. When tea made its Georgian entrance or a sirloin appeared on the menu: 'Why,' Clara was pleased to exclaim, 'this is quite like England!'

Geraldine, fostered in this atmosphere, was tempted in all directions to be exceptional. Each young tendril put out found a wire waiting; she clung and blossomed, while, ambushed in gentleness, Mrs. Letherton-Channing watched like a lynx for the most tentative emanations of young genius. Geraldine was certainly *something*. In preparation for her apotheosis she found herself very much guarded, very much educated, very much petted. There was sometimes a touch of reverence in her step-grandmother's manner. Though the child still danced with anxious clumsiness, sang with a false little clear voice, was listless behind the pencil, nerveless upon the keyboard, heavy upon the bow; her small intellectual flame stooped and wavered; she was docile, but incurious . . . while, in fact, at twelve she could still only claim the divine attribute through that shining vague look and constant abstention from effort in any direction. Nobody was encouraged to contradict Geraldine: it became penal to hurt her feelings. The Beautiful, in all possible concrete forms, was placed about for her contemplation, till life, for her wilful fancy, became an obstacle-race.

Mrs. Letherton-Channing's afternoon visitors — old friends, aware of all this — were relieved on the whole when Geraldine left the room. Talk resumed its usual tenor of indiscretion. The child's presence had been like a flower put down in irrelevant purity alongside one's place at dinner, disconcerting to appetite. 'But what,' murmured a new-comer, a pretty foolish young mother, to Miss Ellis, 'does that poor little creature *do* with herself all day?'

Miss Ellis supposed that the child went into abeyance.

'But has she no governess?'

'Dear me, no: how prosaic!' exclaimed Miss Ellis. The child was no more to her at the moment than a thin little freckled arm.

Geraldine did not go immediately to the library where Mr. Scutcheon, who had come out from Reading to instruct her in Greek, sat biting his nails. Waiting quietly in the hall, she intercepted another slice of the chocolate cake as it was carried out by the butler. She went down the garden: when she had finished her cake and licked her fingers she pulled a rose to pieces, plucking off even the stamens. She eyed the calyx with an obscure sensation of triumph, but had no thoughts. She made gargoyle faces; wishing that she could see herself, she ran to the pool, but the water was clotted with lily-leaves.

'*Old Miss Ellis*,' she said aloud, '*pink as hell is. General Littlecote . . . laughs like a little goat. Lady Miriam Glover . . . hops about like a plover.*' After reflection she added: '*That can't sit on her eggs . . . because of her long legs . . . Geraldine Letherton-Channing . . . ran in and ran in and ran in.*' Then she did run in, judging that Mr. Scutcheon should by now have come to the boil and be cross enough.

She had achieved her purpose. In the library, Mr. Scutcheon, bleak on a background of tooled and gilded book-backs, was furious. The library, with its opulence, revolted him. He was so hungry he could have eaten the books. Mrs. Letherton-Channing never sent in tea: she appeared to believe that tutors were fed by ravens. It was an expensive fancy, that she could easily gratify, to have a step-granddaughter brought up like a Renaissance princess: she paid Mr. Scutcheon an unusually high fee. This in itself tormented his angry and misanthropic honesty, for he considered Geraldine unteachable. At no time did he like teaching the rudiments of his subject; he was unfit, also, for the teaching of young children, for he was impatient and nervous. Geraldine approached Mr. Scutcheon ecstatically, like a martyr approaching a lion.

'You're twenty-five minutes late,' he said snappily.

'Oh, I'm so *sorry*,' she said. 'But perhaps you were early?'

'Exactly: I made a point of being in time. I had been specially anxious to catch the 6.15 home.'

'We saw you come up through the garden: isn't it lovely?'

'A useful short cut,' he said.

He was a thin man, ugly: the very sight of Geraldine set him flushing with irritation just where his pince-nez clipped the bridge of his nose. She glanced at his wrists sticking out of his frayed shirt-cuffs, then at his thin chest. '*Mr. Scutcheon*,' she said to herself, '*never has much on.*' Aloud she added, 'How is your little sister?' His little sister was an invalid.

'Much the same. Now, *please*——' He jerked his chair to the table.

'Do you think I shall ever see her?'

Mr. Scutcheon's sister wilted in a hot room in a hot street, overlooking the tramlines. 'I should think,' he said, 'that is unlikely.' He took quite a sharp displeasure in a picture she wished to present: Geraldine in a white dress on a merciful errand, with a bunch of — say — June lilies, stepping daintily from a car. 'I think,' he said, 'that is unlikely . . . You have crumbs round your mouth,' he added.

'Oh, dear,' fluttered Geraldine. She licked round her lips with the point of her tongue and glanced at him anxiously under her eyelashes. He seemed quite bound up in a resentment she could not fathom. He jerked his wrists further out of his cuffs; the flush on his nose deepened. His anger, his very presence, became delightful. He was the stupidest kind of scholar, without one word to jingle against another. Had he wished, had he dared imperil the flow of Mrs. Letherton-Channing's guineas, he still could not have explained to Geraldine quite what he thought of her: that she was *low*, a sensationalist. He would have agreed that, in *this* sense, Mrs. Letherton-Channing's husband had certainly grandfathered a prodigy.

Geraldine, sighing, took her exercise-books from the table drawer and seated herself beside him. She indicated her work. 'I'm afraid they are not very good,' she said socially, with the air of a lady submitting her drawings to visitors. They were not very good: his furious pencil jabbed and flickered. She caught breath after breath softly, leaning forward beside him. Her soft heavy plaits flopped on to the table: he started irritably. Head almost against his shoulder, she thought comfortably: 'He can't bear me!' She longed to return with Mr. Scutcheon to Reading, a town which — on account of a certain clangour about the streets, a civic rawness, an excess of some quality indigestible by the spirit — Geraldine was seldom allowed to visit.

'I'm not good at anything, am I?' said Geraldine wistfully.

'Possibly you can dance,' replied Mr. Scutcheon. Quartered by silvery ejaculations from the clock, this most interesting hour of Geraldine's week went by too swiftly.

In the rose-clotted loggia, Mrs. Letherton-Channing stood

with Miss Ellis at about seven o'clock. Miss Ellis was staying in the house; the other visitors had departed.

'I think Geraldine's tired; she's not quite herself,' said Mrs. Letherton-Channing.

'Her what?' inquired Miss Ellis, her indulgent cynical pouchy face deepening to coral-pink in the evening glow.

'Not quite herself,' repeated Mrs. Letherton-Channing, who could flatten out any inference. 'I think I shall have to get rid of Mr. Scutcheon. Perhaps she need not do Greek in summer? He has a sulky manner. And, do you know, he has taken to coming up through the garden?'

'Need she do Greek in winter?' said Miss Ellis. 'One could lock the bottom gate,' she added, appreciating the rigours of this unconscious siege.

'But then Miss Weekes could not get out to the village. As it is, she is always too glad of any excuse to come past the house.' Miss Weekes, the resident lady gardener, whose bothy, skilfully planted out by a hedge, was just by the wicket under discussion, remained in outlook resolutely Old English. She whistled; the smock and breeches in which she worked were an offence to Mrs. Letherton-Channing, who had engaged her to look after the frames and hot-houses, not expecting her to emerge from these. She had discovered that Miss Weekes morris-danced, that she did rush-work, that she participated in every possible movement to build Jerusalem in this pleasant and green part of Berkshire. At no moment, when off duty, did Miss Weekes, darting here and there through the village, apparently cease from mental strife. Mrs. Letherton-Channing could countenance a diluted reality but could not suffer a fellow fantasist. The woman was, moreover, unfriendly to Geraldine. It was clear that Miss Weekes *must* have let Mr. Scutcheon in through the lower gate. But she had a wonderful way with asparagus.

'It is difficult,' sighed Mrs. Letherton-Channing.

'It must be,' agreed Miss Ellis.

Mrs. Letherton-Channing did not find her friend's satirical manner at all disconcerting. The appearance of Geraldine's step-grandmother was fine, even noble; she had presence, her white waved hair fitted her head like a cap. Her dark prominent eyes looked out at any margin of world beyond the domain of her own massive fancy without prejudice, almost without recognition. The mood of a d'Este princess dominated her interviews with the very cook. She was generous, and, feeling indebted to Geraldine's mother by her death, now spoke of her kindly. An etherealized grand-maternity, without the awkward preliminaries of mother-hood, became her excellently; just as widowhood, after the exigencies of marriage, was at once the harbour and crown of her spirit. Her hands wrinkled slightly at the wrists like white kid gloves.

Miss Ellis, suddenly bored with composing a picture of ladies in a rosy sunset loggia, said innocently: 'I see in Gerald-ine now and then quite a touch of poor Vivien's manner. The real pretty woman's curtness.'

Mrs. Letherton-Channing smiled. 'To me,' she said, 'she is like nobody but herself.'

'She'll meddle with life,' said Clara. She struck with her cushiony fingers several staccato chords on the stone balus-trade of the loggia. 'I can't think,' she exclaimed, 'how they do it!'

'They?'

'Women — how they ever bring up their own children!'

Mrs. Letherton-Channing pulled off one or two dead roses. 'Look how they fail,' she said placidly.

For less than a minute Geraldine's supper — the green goblet of milk, the Romary biscuits, the glossy strawberry-pyramid on a plate like a leaf — attracted Geraldine's eye, her look dark with secrecy, with some conspiracy with herself. Then she turned from it, pressing a strawberry to her bunched-up lips that slowly yielded as the fruit flattened and sweet red juice ran down her chin. 'The Enemies . . .' she said aloud, in a tone of exaltation and terror, 'the *Enemies*!'

She was alone in her room, that, softly pale-pink and full of friendly light from the garden, seemed to be enclosed by more than material walls, by volutions of delicacy and sweet living shadows: the inner whorl of a shell, the heart of a flower. If stone sustained it, the very stone was kind. Here was the secret form of her little-girlhood, tenderly animate by the spirit. Here, round the smiling gold clock, time was captive, and only fluttered with little moth-wings; here, coming in, you distilled the whole sweetness of youth from a happy consciousness of mortality: the narrow bed was innocent as an early grave. By falling asleep here, the little girl gave herself back to the centuries, to touch, from their heart, the very heart of your fancy, like a little girl in an epitaph.

Geraldine's room had been furnished with discrimination. Botticelli wildflowers were woven into the curtains, garlands were painted over the furniture, and, on the bed-head, a fanciful picture of a sailing-ship. Over the bed hung a panel of leafy Perugian damask: at eye-level, opposite, Carpaccio's little St. Ursula lay flat and calmly; even an angel did not disturb her, she was the very picture of afternoon sleep. Trees looked in at St. Ursula's window: from Geraldine's window you saw the flagged path dropping terrace by terrace and the young tips of cypresses.

But here (you might notice) vacant little Geraldine seemed to exist with difficulty. Every time her reflection flitted out of the looking-glass the whole of Geraldine seemed to become mislaid. A huge rubber ball balanced on top of the bureau, Geraldine's stockings straggled over a chair; every day she trod biscuit-crumbs into the carpet. The air smelt faintly of peppermint, from her tooth-powder. Otherwise this was a guest-room: ready, but someone never arrived.

'The enemies . . .' she repeated. And at this evocation the pale walls contracted, the air darkened. With that soft creak of her sandals, pulling and pulling at the strawberry with her lips, Geraldine paced round that group of Imaginary Furious People occupying the centre of her floor.

They had just come in.

Mr. Scutcheon, one of her grandmother's roses stuck defiantly into his button-hole, put in his nightly appearance. Miss Weekes, her hands in her breeches pockets, looked at Geraldine meditatively and contemptuously. Two more of her teachers were there, also the Angry Woman from the Village, the Little Boy from the Lodge, and, oddly enough, her own mother, who seemed to have some understanding with all the rest. (It was eight o'clock; downstairs, Mrs. Letherton-Channing and Miss Ellis sat down to dinner.) In the enchanted half-light the Enemies stood glancing darkly at one another, urging each other on.

Geraldine, in elation, threw away the calyx of the strawberry. 'What do you want?' she whispered.

'*We've come*,' said Mr. Thorne, who taught Geraldine mathematics. All the rest murmured.

'You must go,' she said haughtily.

'*We don't think*,' said the Little Boy from the Lodge, with an ugly look, while Miss Weekes, never taking her awful eyes from Geraldine, began to feel about for something in her pocket.

'*It's all up, Geraldine*,' said her mother, who seemed less interested, more indifferent than the rest, and wore her old ironical smile. All the same, she *had* some part in this, for

Geraldine understood that in the last four years, since her mother died, the two had become strangers. Geraldine knotted her hands behind her and thrust her chin up.

'*There has been the Revolution*,' said Mr. Scutcheon. The Enemies, drawing closer behind him, nodded. Geraldine saw them look round at the things about the room, wondering which to seize first. On Greek days, Mr. Scutcheon was always promoted to be their leader. His eyes were bloodshot; he was wearing a black fur cap and carried a bottle. Evidently pistols were in his pocket. (Geraldine's fancy could hardly do more for anyone.)

'*Reading is running red with Blood*,' added Mr. Thorne, who was nearly as vindictive. Geraldine, however, did not see him so plainly; his rage was inferior. '*And as for London . . .*' went on Mr. Thorne.

'*Hush*,' said Miss Weekes, but with a greedy look, as though she had been dwelling on this a long time. She took her pruning-knife from her pocket and turned it over.

Geraldine's mother said again with detachment, '*It's all up, Geraldine.*'

'*Mrs. Letherton-Channing is loaded with chains*,' said the music mistress, who had at present a difficulty with her manner. For by day Miss Snipe's manner was at once obsequious and regretful: as an Enemy it was hard for her to behave. But Geraldine, glancing sidelong at her during a music lesson, as they sat elbow to elbow before the piano, had once seen her eyes go watery with malevolence. Miss Snipe, though wearing a fur cap, now appeared scared by success, and resentful, as though she felt she did not fully enjoy her triumph.

'*As for you——*' began Mr. Thorne. The Enemies' heads went together: the Angry Woman nodded. A delicious anticipation mounted in Geraldine.

Geraldine's mother glanced quizzically at the Enemies, but seemed, all the same, a little displeased by her strange company and their intention. So she had that same old smile, as much as to say, 'But what can one do?' During these years of death she must have forgotten all loving pity, as Geraldine had forgotten it. Each unspoken word by which Mrs. Letherton-Channing estranged further mother and daughter must have been heard by the mother, who now returned each night with the Enemies, always a little colder, to her lost unfaithful child.

When the Enemies all moved forward steadily, resolute as one face, Geraldine's feeling took on such violence that even the birds became silent outside the window. Geraldine's excitement, courted with every sense, became unbearable. Through the dark flanks of the crowd she saw with ecstatic despair her goblet of milk, always waiting, solid and pale. She asked, 'General Littlecote?': they replied: '*He is massacred too.*' She saw his foolish old face lie in blood on a staircase, and spread out her hand to her side, in terror, close to her thumping heart. Her cheeks blazed. The rope of excitement she had been playing out guardedly, sparingly, now fled through her fingers, burning. She began to shout '*I defy*——!' and stamped on the mild carpet. (Downstairs, over the heads of Mrs. Letherton-Channing, so placidly dining, and Miss Ellis, the chandelier blinked and tinkled.) Her Enemies, like a bubble swelling and darkening, a Menace beyond dimensions, Genii glaring and towering, showed how they would advance inch by inch with knives gleaming. . . .

Geraldine dropped with a bump to her bare knees under their rush. . . .

.   .   .   .   .   .

Geraldine got up from her knees, whistling, flushed, considerably embarrassed. She picked up the goblet and drank, bubbling into the milk: as she drank she glanced round the room as though it had been another child's nursery. The looking-glasses were innocent. There was now something about her at once cold and cryptic: she was thankful to be alone. She was, in fact, for herself a most unfriendly playmate, for she was treacherous. There remained, however, something in the air of the room that did not at once clear or dissolve or settle as dust settles, though the white drugget where *they* had all stood remained unwrinkled. There was still not quite silence after this nightly session of the red passions.

Mrs. Letherton-Channing never entered her granddaughter's room without pleasure: pleasure shared or reflected tonight, for Miss Ellis accompanied her. They wore teagowns: their bodies, massive pillars of flesh, were softened about the outline and great wings of chiffon rose up with every gesture. Between them Geraldine lay curled in her bed sideways, a hand under her cheek.

'Somebody's tired,' said Mrs. Letherton-Channing, stooping over the bed.

'Somebody's got a milky moustache,' said Miss Ellis.

Geraldine wiped her mouth.

Mrs. Letherton-Channing stooped lower to look into Geraldine's eyes, which, as the child lay looking up, were exposed like pools to her. 'There's nothing you don't like . . .?'

'Dear me,' said her friend, with satirical softness, 'we're all human.'

Mrs. Letherton-Channing took no notice. Moving softly, heavily, in her tea-gown, like something run on castors over the floor, she opened the window wider, to ask more night in. She put a bowl of flowers outside the door: by night flowers were enemies. Her own idea of peace filled the room: the child's bed became the very image of sleep. (Her own sleep came in tablets out of a bottle.) Night between these colourless walls became as spacious and pure as a sky, in which her own solid form and Clara's seemed miraculously to be suspended.

Even Miss Ellis, her face close to Geraldine, whispered: 'I wish I were your age!'

'Do you?'

It became clear to Geraldine (as she lay, without curiosity, eyes fixed on the curves of Miss Ellis's chin) — from the two ladies' manner and circumspect breathing, from the sound of wicker chairs being carried in from the terrace, from the gramophone jigging a dance, very faint, down in Miss Weekes's bothy, from, through trees, the sickle of light from a car that made the rest of the sky so suddenly dark — that the red Revolution was still delayed. Security, feeling for her in the dark, closed the last of its tentacles on her limbs, her senses. When the door shut, when they had gone, she sighed acquiescence into her frilly pillow and once more slept in her prison.

FIRELIGHT IN THE FLAT

BOB ROBERTSON, sore from the morning's row with his wife, came home warily, step after step reluctantly up the fibre-carpeted stairs — the flats had no lift — with a stop on each of the floors as though his breath had morally given out.

Here, six floors up, was his door: red shone through the frosted panels where a strip of firelight reached over the hall.

Rattling the key in, he felt the lock slip round. Then — for the hall was jasminy with her scent — he tentatively called: 'Betty?' Before there was time for an answer, he felt her absence. She had gone out, certainly: she would be at the flicks. 'Damn,' said Robertson flatly. He'd meant to make things all right. This was what intentions came to. He hung up his hat in the dark.

Robertson was an ex-officer; as the war kept receding, this counted for less and less. Still, on the strength of this and of a school that was almost public, he travelled in high-class etchings and educational prints. His wife, Betty, bought shiny courageous stockings in bargain basements and regretted to friends that they could not afford children. Life disheartened her, really, and more and more of their food came back cooked from the *delikatessen* in paper bags.

Now the walls jumped in and out of shadow: a five-shilling clock struck a half-hour long ago past. Far down below, the traffic went past in jerks to the Great West Road, as though being pumped out of London. The sitting-room

137

door was confidentially open: two armchair-backs, against the red waning fire, took off, somehow, one's idea of a home. Dull with patent fuelling, but in Mother's tradition, the open fire kept something inside alight. Bitterly retrospective, Robertson reached out for the switch. But there was no electricity. He felt round in his pocket: he had no shilling.

'Good Lord: *Bobbet!*' said Constance, turning in an armchair.

'Good *Lord!*' he replied, shaken. 'Constance? Don't do that again!'

'I was asleep.'

'Got a shilling?'

'No, spent it. I've got Betty's latchkey; she's with Diane. I'm waiting here to borrow my bus fare home.'

'You are the limit,' said he, and, having discovered her face looking up at him, kissed it — which was their way.

'Steady,' said she, rearranging the curl on her forehead. She was about seventeen.

'Got that job yet?'

'What *do* you expect?' said Constance sardonically.

'Better get married.'

'Oh, naturally,' agreed Constance. 'But, then, as I always say . . .' She didn't, however, say it. He sat down in the other armchair, stretched out his legs, and sighed. 'You know,' he confided, 'I wasn't a bit keen, really, on getting back here this evening. Funny, wasn't it?'

Constance quite understood. Knees crossed, she swung one foot happily in the firelight. 'All you men are the same, all boys, really. You don't know what you want till you think you're not getting it.'

'I and Betty had a dust-up.' (She half listened, quite calmly.) 'You know, she's impossible, Constance; if I never say it again. It's really a bit stiff sometimes. Of course, I know things come hard on her. But she does muddle about so.' This was just; all day long she went clicking about the flat in those high-heeled old satin slippers with straps undone. She would crouch in front of the grate and groan at the messy grey ashes. He knew what was wrong with Betty: she wanted a gas fire. All day long she would sigh that she was done in.

'I wish you could see my fingers,' said Constance suddenly. 'I've just had a manicure.'

'Show!' She put her hands close to the fire; the nails glistened: they both bent over them.

'You are a funny kid, Constance.'

'Shut up.' She licked a finger and stamped three ripples back again on her forehead. 'You know,' she resumed, 'what I feel about a manicure: it does pull you together. I know a place where men come in to be manicured — wouldn't that make you sick!'

'It's snug sitting here in the dark. Just you and I, Constance . . . You don't know what I miss.'

'Bobbet, look here: I'm hungry,' she interrupted.

'So am I, damned hungry.' Robertson leaned towards Constance, across the fire, knocking his knuckles together between his knees. 'Do you know,' he said passionately, 'it's a year since I've had roast mutton? Betty won't touch cooking. All this muck out of paper bags—'

'Well, she does at least hot up things from the *delikatessen*. I should get stuff out of tins — you know, salmon. I suppose you haven't got any salmon here?'

He went to see; she followed; he struck matches; laughing they groped their way to the kitchenette. He dropped spent matches; she stamped them carefully out. Here was a half pork pie, chiefly pastry, there three split peaches floating syrupy in a Woolworth dish; some biscuits — one was nibbled along the edge. They laughed. But the food smelled strong in the close air; there was a smell of old gas from the cooker. All delicate fingertips, Constance fished up a peach, leaning forward to let the syrup drip clear of her tight black frock. He watched: flame crept unnoticed up the match to his fingers. He swore sharply; they were in the dark. They followed each other by touch, till a pale fluctuation of firelight led them back to the hall. Robertson had brought the pork pie with him.

'But Betty'll be coming in,' he said gloomily.

'Well, what of it? But she won't; not till eight. She and Diane went in about half-past five; they'll be seeing the programme round.' She knelt to poke the fire, making it light the room up. Then her voice changed to an odd note. I say . . . do you ever have any money?'

'Bus fare? Don't go yet, there's a good girl.'

'No, but I want some money: a good deal.'

'Marry money,' he said, intent on what he was at. He had settled down with the pie balanced on one knee and was hacking away at the crust with a pocket-knife. Constance's silence, her placid watching and waiting, suddenly filled the room: in fancy he saw a table pulled up to a window, a dish of gooseberries (why, he could not think), and, out there in the country dusk, high poplars vaguely and gravely swaying. The scene, in a sphere of desire, was round and perfect. So one would live if one kept a chicken farm. 'Marry money,' he went on waggishly, still intent. But he put out a hand for Constance's.

'But, you damn fool,' cried Constance, starting up very suddenly, standing beside the door and clicking the impotent switch up and down, up and down. 'I need money *now*. I want it at once — can't you *see?*'

He was unnerved by her outburst, as though a cold wind snatched open the doors of the flat. He contracted into himself, defensive and unfriendly. She had ruined their fun; he wished she would shut up. 'See?' he repeated, dividing the pie accurately. 'No, I don't specially see. We all want money like that.'

Her high heel rapped the floor. 'But I must have it now. Do you have to be told point-blank? I've got to get right out — *soon*.' Her heel stopped and she stood desperately still.

With a dull shock he understood, and said under his breath: '*Constance!*'

'Oo-er, you wicked girl,' said Constance, with hopeless frivolity. 'Go on: consider it said.'

Uneasy — for to what extent had she not already imposed on him? — and with rising anger, he said, 'But why in hell's name come to *me*? . . . Anyway,' he added quickly, 'I've *got* no money. And if I had, my girl, think what Betty might think.'

'My mistake,' said Constance. 'It just occurred to me. As we seemed to be getting along so well. I've got to *get* that money, so any port in a storm.'

'So you thought it was worth trying?' Exasperated by her contemptuous lightness, her irony, and this net of doom she was casting about the flat, he glared in the firelight at his portion of pie. She had ruined his appetite. At last he could say more gently: 'What did you do it for?'

'New clothes,' said Constance loudly.

'Get out of here, you little——!'

'Yes, all right,' she said. 'I'm going.'

'No, look here. Stop. Do for God's sake be decent with me. I'm not down on you, but I'm damned if I'll stand your attitude. Whatever possessed you, you little fool?'

'I suppose I was balmy,' said Constance, turning away.

'Love?' he said, uneasy.

'I said, I suppose I was balmy . . . Only Bobbet, look here, don't keep going on about marriage. Because it makes you sound silly now, doesn't it?'

'But I don't see why you shouldn't,' he said eagerly. 'I'd marry you ... there'd be heaps of men; all men aren't such swine. *I'd* marry you,' he repeated, with a growing security.

'I wouldn't marry *you*,' said Constance. 'Not for anything, now. Not if it had *been* you: I'd rather walk into the Serpentine. Thanks all the same.'

'Oh, well,' he said, and added, not quite in irony: 'But it's been a nice evening, hasn't it?'

'Well then, listen,' she said. 'What about that money, really? You needn't worry: I swear you'll get it back. I'll want about fifty pounds: I think I could manage on that. Will you or won't you? I've got no time to be sweet.'

'Well ...' he began. Because, when you come to think of it ... because after all ... 'The thing is——' he began again, with a frankness that should have won her. 'Well, you see how I *stand*. I've got Betty to think of.'

'Yes, you don't half think of Betty!'

'Well, damn it all, she's my wife——'

'Lucky girl!'

'I must say, Constance, you're a very poor gold-digger!'

She said drearily: 'I've never tried before.'

'What about — whoever it was?'

'I'd rather walk into the Serpentine.'

'Blast!' he said. 'You spoil everything.' And he sat huddled forward, his head in his hands. For, really, there seemed no peace for him anywhere. He did simply want a woman to cheer him up. Betty was weak and Constance was bad right through.

'Sorry I came?' she said, groping round for her hat.

He sat on, scrubbing his fingers up through his hair.

'It's no good about the money?' She listened, he listened; the fire snapped. 'Right-oh,' she said, 'I'm off.'

'I'll think out something,' he said. 'I'll write in a day or two. I swear I'll see you through——'

At this point, Betty, having lent Constance her latchkey, was forced to ring at the door of her own flat. She rang twice, eager to be at home. As Robertson sat on, stupefied, Constance went to the door.

'Hullo, Con,' he heard Betty greet her. 'Find your way in all right?'

'Yep. Bobbet's back. I've been trying to borrow money.'

'*I* don't know what you're thinking of,' Betty said languidly. '*We* don't have any money ... Hullo, Bobbet ... Hullo,' what's up with the light?'

'We're right out of shillings.'

'Here are three in the cigarette-box; there're always some there. We're not so broke as you'd think,' Betty said, laughing, to Constance. 'How much do *you* want, Con?'

'Sixpence — I want my bus fare.'

'Well, take a shilling.'

Betty clinked the shilling into the meter. The flat sprang into sight: 'art' distemper, six of The World's Best Pictures, the dark sharp angles of antiqued oak. Constance strolled to a glass and made up her mouth scarlet, then pulled on her tight little hat with the jockey brim. She wrapped up her chin in her collar. 'I must be pushing along,' she said. 'Thanks for the shilling.'

'Sorry, darling, we can't keep you to supper. But the fact is, I don't think the galantine ...'

'I must get along, anyhow; mother'll be raging. 'Sides, I've had some pig pie.'

'Splendid. Go on, Bobbet, go to the door with her!'

When he came back from the door, Robertson saw at once

how battered Betty was looking. The fact was, she couldn't
get on without him; she curled up under his anger and went to
bits. She must have been crying, for the mascara had run
right round her eyes. Now she was fluffing her hair up, for
him specially. He could not know that her throat, under the
tight pink pearls, was burning just at a point where the Die-
trich's throat had been kissed some minutes before. Her fox
fur slid off one shoulder, she sat just where Constance had sat,
looking up at him. 'Oh, *Bobbet*,' she said, 'I've been so—oh, I
don't know. But I do get so fed up.'

'Poor girl,' he said, touching her cheek. She sighed and
caught at his hand, and sat fondling it, with her head back on
his arm and her long lashes turned down. 'I feel rotten, she
said, 'about everything.'

'Oh, well . . . You've been washing your hair.'

'Look at my pearls; Swan & Edgar: two and eleven-three.
Was I awful? I had to have something.'

'I like you to have pretty things.'

'Yes, you *are* a sweet about that.'

'Constance is a funny girl,' she said later. 'So independent
— I can't make her out. Did you talk much?'

'Not particularly.'

'I'm sorry for her in a way — oh, the fire's nearly out.' The
fire, indeed, had gone dull in the brilliant glare. One had had,
thought Robertson, half-heartedly poking it, quite enough
of all that.

'It's wasted,' he said, 'when we're out. Blazing away all the
time. How would it really be if we *had* a gas fire?'

'Oh, but I love the firelight: it's so homey. It's just doing
the grate—— Still, I do love the firelight.'

'How would it be,' he said, 'if we cleared right out of all this
and started a chicken farm? I've got that bit saved. I'm just as
fed up as you are. You know, in the country somewhere.'

'*Bobbet* — and a sweet cottage?'

They held hands to think of it: he thought of huts and chickens, she thought of children. A country silence crept into the flat: outside, there might have been poplars, vaguely and gravely swaying. They felt oddly secure.

'You and me. We've never had much of a break.'

'It's funny,' she said on their way to bed that night, 'the way that girl Constance never has the price of a bus fare, I often wonder what will become of her. . . .'

THE MAN OF THE FAMILY

'DEAR WILLIAM,' Mrs. Peel kept exclaiming. '*Isn't* William wonderful?' She was his Aunt Luella, and because his talk was beyond her, and she could not always grasp what he was saying, she kept casting bright sceptical glances around the lunch-table. Her blonde shell-rimmed spectacles gave these glances a twinkle. Lady Lambe, his Aunt Héloïse, however, listened intently; she made little flapping gestures at the butler when he offered her things, as though she could not bear to be distracted. When she noticed the *soufflé* the others were eating she recalled the butler with an apology.

After each interruption William would raise his voice half a tone and continue patiently. He was on his way across London from Oxford. Patsey, beside him, sat with her hands on her lap twisting her rings about when she was not eating and taking no part in the talk. She was not modern at all and always seemed discouraged. Pretty Rachel sat smiling into the bowl of glass fruit, on which green sunshine, reflected back from the Regent's Park trees, twinkled and slid. The trees were in full June light, the dining-room in shadow. The table was round, with no 'head', so that any difficulty in placing William had been avoided.

Aunt Héloïse was also a Liberal: at the last three elections she had stood for Parliament: she meant to keep on standing. She was not original, but she was sound and receptive; when she came down to Oxford he took her to debates at the Union.

Rachel Lambe never came with her mother; she said they all made her feel so terribly old (she was twenty-four). He too seldom saw her; she went out a great deal and seemed to have numerous friends; when they met she, though so naive, contrived to be very mysterious. She had bronzy-gold hair, parted down the centre, that rippled smoothly against the line of her cheeks, and a smile — subtle, gentle, malicious — that sent curves up under her eyes: a da Vinci smile. An extraordinary daughter for one of one's aunts to have had.

William always lunched at his Aunt Luella's on his way across London. The Regent's Park house was his *pied-à-terre*; he could put up here even when the family were out of town, and bring friends in to meals — had he wished. Aunt Luella was an irritating, attractive woman; she was thin as a lath, wore a perpetual string of brown amber, and dressed to tone in with it. Her taste in interior decoration made him blush, but she kept an excellent table. She called him 'the man of the family' or 'the head of the family' (which he in fact was), and scoffed away gently at him. She scoffed at herself, her daughter and everyone else. Patsey was thirty-two, and looked like her mother's sister. She was statuesque, expensively dressed, and null; she had been engaged twice, but nothing had come of it. Quite a lot of life (he often longed to point out) was before her; interests still offered, but Patsey seemed blind to them. Her tomboyish name was unsuitable; Patsey was painfully womanly.

When William and Aunt Héloïse had settled the Government finally, they cleared their throats and there was a benign pause. Aunt Luella blinked. The butler came round with the Camembert. 'Do they *teach* you politics at Oxford?' Rachel said vaguely. William did not reply; he readjusted himself and turned sideways to Patsey.

'Well, Patsey, how goes it?' he said at last, genially.

She started violently. 'Goes what?' she said, flustered. 'It? Oh, very well, thank you. I've been having a lovely time.'

'Good,' said William. 'Splendid.'

'I've been helping at fêtes,' Patsey explained conscientiously. 'I went to the Chelsea Flower Show. I've been ever so many times to the Academy.'

'Splendid,' said William drearily. 'Nothing like going around. A man I know meant to go to the Academy only the other day, but I don't think he ever did.'

She looked at him, sidelong, out of her doglike brown eyes.

'I *adore* the Academy,' Rachel put in in her deep voice. 'I went to the private view and saw everyone. I *adore* the Academy.'

'Rachel "adores" anything to do with clothes,' said her mother. It was gratifying to her, as a plain intellectual woman to have produced something so pretty and frivolous. Yet neither 'pretty' nor 'frivolous' suited Rachael; they hung foolishly as pink muslin on her queer personality.

'Aren't I futile?' said Rachel, smiling down at her peach.

There certainly was no brandy like Aunt Luella's. William slid back in his chair with a good feeling inside. Catching her eye, be bowed an acknowledgment. 'And, oh, *William*,' said she, leaning suddenly forward. 'If you're not too busy today I'd love a little talk some time. Business.'

Business was Aunt Luella's forte. She loved to settle down at it for a stretch and bemuse William with documents. In her morning-room, with gold curtains and beetle-green walls blistered over with bluish patches like scum on a pool, he had put in hours of claustrophobia and torment. The shining shagreen accoutrements of her desk disappeared early under a sea of parchments — deeds, securities, settlements — God could hardly know what. Dispatch-boxes yawned and pink tape littered the floor. When he was of age she meant him to be a

Trustee — he felt even now she was fattening him up for one. She ran in and out of documents like a spider, at demoniacal speed. 'Of course,' she would say, 'I've really no *head* for these things. One's a lone woman — but don't let me bother you. Only it is such a help to talks thing out with a man. Your father was marvellous; no one could know what a help to me! But you must be *sure* now and don't let me waste your time.'

Escape was always impossible. 'I wish I took after father,' William would mutter, scrubbing his hands through his hair.

'I think you've a *wonderful* grasp of things,' she would always say brightly. These were the only occasions when she took him — or anything — seriously. He never could think what the woman thought she was getting at — showing off, merely? He could bet any amount she hadn't allowed Uncle Henry within sight of those boxes; she had so thoroughly kept Uncle Henry down. William hated, however, to be a beast in any way about Aunt Luella.

This afternoon, however, no tin boxes appeared. She burrowed vaguely in one writing-table drawer, giving William time to finish his coffee and light one more of her excellent cigarettes. He wondered sadly if Rachel would have gone by the time she had finished; he had thought it might be pleasant to walk back with Rachel across the Park. He jumped when Aunt Luella, twisting round on her chair, leaned vivaciously towards him and, swinging out her string of beads on one finger, said: 'It's about *Patsey*. Didn't you notice her?'

'N-not particularly.'

'She's been looking really quite brilliant. The thing is: Patsey's just going to be engaged again — I don't say *married*, because really I'm getting so superstitious about the poor darling. Engaged. Well, she is now, really, only I mean it isn't announced.'

'How terribly nice,' said William, clattering down his coffee-cup. 'Shall I go and congratulate her?'

'*Just* one moment . . . He's really, the dearest old charming thing; "Chummy," we call him — his name's Everard. So *nice*, so nice-looking, such nice people. Patsey and I are delighted with him. It's ideal — just one thing's a pity. He is divorced, poor dear.'

'Oh . . . Did it, or had it done to him?'

'Oh, *did* it, of course. The wife was a little baggage. He's been worn to a shadow, had no sort of life. He wants somebody absolutely reposeful. Patsey's the very thing. It's lovely to see them together. Only people do ask such silly questions, and talk. "Wasn't he divorced?" they say, as if poor Chummy hadn't come out of it splendidly. So I just thought I'd tell you before you spoke to Patsey, so's you couldn't ask anything awkward. Not that you would. We're all quite full of it — Aunt Héloïse, Rachel, and all. Only do remember, it isn't really *announced*.'

Up in the Chinese drawing-room, Patsey and Rachel sat one at each end of a sofa, each glancing over a copy of *Vogue*. Rachel had the more recent. Aunt Héloïse sat in an upright chair by the window reading *The Times* thoroughly. Patsey kept re-settling her cushions behind her, and Rachel re-crossing her legs; the room was full of the amiable drooping silence of relatives who have nothing special to say. When William entered, all three of them brightened up. Rachel leaned back with her hands propping her head; Patsey, pinkly self-conscious, shuffled *Vogue* off her knee, then pulled it back and began to scan the advertisements.

William, congratulations nicely delivered, stayed looming above them, hands in his pockets. Rachel meanwhile gazed up at him, not unkindly. He was a nice-looking fairish youth, intelligent but bothered-looking. He had even some prestige; his own friends thought he disproved that one couldn't be brilliant *and* solid. 'I shall hope to meet Everard,' he was saying to Patsey encouragingly. He remembered how, centuries ago, when he was still at his prep school, Patsey had come down one afternoon in the car, very much engaged, very pink, very conscious, with her first young man, Gerald, very pink also. She seemed to be nearly always in this condition. 'Chummy's coming to tea,' she said proudly, with that old deprecating, absurd, rather touching glow in her cheeks. 'You *will* stay, won't you? I thought we might all get tickets for something tomorrow night.'

'Um-m,' said William. He glanced at Rachel — it rather depended on her. But Rachel did not respond: he was disconcerted at catching a flash of glances across him. Rachel and Rachel's mother were making faces — or something subtler: 'expressions' — at one another.

'I'm terribly much afraid,' he said, scenting danger, 'I can't be in town for more than a night this time. I'm so sorry, Patsy. But I'd love to stay for tea.'

Rachel could not stay for tea: she was seldom available. She must get back she said; she had some wretched people coming. Aunt Héloïse had a committee meeting at three. Lady Lambe had four afternoon committees a week, and on those afternoons Rachel was at home to friends. Lady Lambe and her daughter lived in Walpole Street, Chelsea. Rachel, getting up thoughtfully, invited William to walk just across the Park with her. 'I think Regent's Park's so shady; one never knows. Last time I got spoken to by a boy on a scooter, and today I was followed by a repulsive Airedale. We parted out on the doorstep; it's probably waiting still. I hate dogs, you know.'

'Oh, poor old fellow,' cried Patsey; 'he must have got lost!'

Rachel thought this quite likely; she patted the top of Patsey's head, kissed her hand to her mother, and went out, followed by William, who felt pleased.

Rachel walked beautifully; people kept turning to look at her. Her blue dress fled back from her figure in the light wind and the waves of her gold hair flickered against her cheeks. William wore the grey flannels and brown hat in which he had left Oxford. He decided that if Rachel should happen to ask him to come back to tea with her, Chummy might well keep. She walked in an absent silence, but he felt she had something special to say. He glanced at her once or twice, then said at a venture: 'What do *you* think of this person — this Everard?'

She looked past him at the lake and said casually, 'I *don't* think about him, but I know him, of course.'

'Oh, you do? Doesn't he bear thinking about?'

'Oh, I don't know whether he'd *bear* it — he's just not worth the effort. I don't think often.'

'Aunt Luella and Pat seem pleased.'

'Yes, poor dears,' agreed Rachel, and wrinkled up her nose. 'Aren't women all pathetic?'

This had not struck him. 'So long as *they're* pleased,' he said, 'I don't think we need think twice of it. Patsey's obviously got to marry someone.'

'Oh, I know,' agreed Rachael. 'Babies and that sort of thing. But she can't, I'm afraid, marry Chummy — so this has got to be stopped.'

William pulled up short; his mind reeled. Rachel came to a stop too, and stood eyeing him calmly.

'Why on earth? What's the matter with it? Or do *you* want to marry him?'

This sounded unkind, but seemed to him only fair. Such

awkward clashes often occurred in novels. But Rachel shook her head definitely 'Though I'd do quite a lot,' she said, 'for a really good home. But that, as a matter of fact, is exactly what Everard's after himself. I don't want to sound a brute, you know, William, but of course Aunt Luella and Patsey are very well off: what you'd call "warm". Everard values his comforts. After the first lunch he must have seen points about Patsey, and after two or three dinners and door-to-doors in the Daimler the best of her really nice character must have been perfectly clear. I don't mean that he probably isn't quite fond of her by this time — who wouldn't be, of Patsey? She's the dearest old slug.'

'Still, if they're both pleased,' William repeated. 'And, after all, people have to have *some* reason to marry. Aunt Luella may not be strong as a mother, but she's a born mother-in-law. Think what a time Chummy'll have with those black boxes!'

'That's just it. The poor woman's such a hopeless fool about money. She's as timid as a fowl by herself, and wouldn't re-invest tuppence, but she's probably been chatting to him about securities and he'll have been telling her she's the perfect woman of business. You know how weak her head is. I wouldn't mind him messing Aunt Luella's money about and losing it for her — she's got far too much — if he weren't also going to mess up Patsey's affections. But I cannot see why any one man should do both.'

Rachel said this so weightily that he stared.

'Do you hate him?' he asked. 'Or just know him fearfully well?'

'Wellish,' said Rachel. 'At least, I suppose you might say so. We nearly went abroad.'

They walked at uneven speed in the shade of the beeches, heads close for discretion's sake and talking in low tones.

People veered to avoid them, for they looked anxious and pretty, like a young couple in love. Even William's friends, had they passed, might have thought this of him. Rachel paused at an empty seat and looked down at it hopelessly; William dusted a patch with his handkerchief and they both sat down. He stuck his feet out and glared at the toes of his shoes. Rachel brought out a mirror, studied her mouth, and applied a little more red.

'It was when I first grew up,' she said. 'I was fearfully bored. You know how hard up we were till grandfather died. Mother'd dropped all her friends who weren't on the right committees, and I never saw anyone, and had nothing to wear if I did. Mother never thought about anything but saving European children, and I used to take pleats in Patsey's cast-offs and wish I could die. Everyone seemed to be having a marvellous time, though I don't suppose they were really. Then a girl asked me down at the last moment to fill up a gap in a Hunt Ball party; Aunt Luella stood me a frock and I easily picked up Everard. I thought I was made.

'He seemed to be quite an experience. I had always suspected I must be all right really, but I never quite knew how nice I could be. He hadn't then come to the end of his wife's money, so he gave me a slap-up time. I wasn't a bit particular in those days. I saw he had mouldy patches, but that didn't bother me, till I met somebody else – but I hadn't then. Then he said, "Come abroad," and I didn't see why not. I'm sorry, William, but morals are like clothes and I'd scrapped one lot and hadn't found others to suit me. He said we'd go in his car. Mother was going to Serbia on a hunt of some kind. We fixed our start for the day after she was going – three weeks ahead. But in those three weeks Everard lost colour. One way and another . . . His wife put him on an allowance, and he got careful – not to say slightly morbid if he thought he was spending too much. So when he did take one out, he wanted his money's worth. He's not stupid, exactly; he's got a tongue. That's where I went right off him. In fact, he's not a nice man. That's where Patsey's heart would come in. You may think me cynical, William, but I honestly do believe that manners (or people not having them) undermine happiness far quicker than morals. A person, specially not a person like Patsey, can't expect her husband always to stay in her pocket, but she does expect him to be polite when he's there. It's these little remarks with an edge — you know, spiteful, cutting. He'd skin Patsey alive. He can't leave a person in peace once he doesn't like their face or thinks they're not keen on his. He never *hurt* me: you see, I wasn't really attached to him; but he merely annoyed me rather. I "kept him under observation" (as they say about measles), and when, the very last day, he turned nasty at having to pay an extra seven-and-six on my passport, I simply went home. I went down to Aunt Luella in Wales and wired from there that our trip was off, on grounds of economy.

'Now mind you, William, those three weeks he was in love with me and wanting me more than anything, and still he couldn't help being nasty. What he's wanting now is the key to Aunt Luella's black boxes — and, I daresay, the key of the cellar. What chance has Patsey got once they've settled him in?'

'You mean,' said William anxiously, 'that there's a distinction between being nasty and being simply immoral?'

'I do, of course,' said Rachel, with some impatience. 'Now you do see why this marriage is impossible?'

Her recital had given William all sorts of queer feelings. However, he felt he knew Rachel very much better. His theory that this sort of thing only happened to other people's

156

relations broke down. 'What a lot goes on,' he thought. 'And how calmly women take it.' He felt Rachel underrated his own sex. All the same, he had this new, intimate feeling about her. 'But I can't quite see what you're going to do,' he said.

'It's a question of what you are going to do,' she said. 'You see, you will be expected to take a line about this.'

'My dear girl——'

'Why else do you think I told you?' said Rachel languidly, opening her eyes very wide.

'What do you expect me to do?' he asked. 'Rush back and kick Everard, shouting "Swine, swine, swine, swine?"'

Sitting with hands folded on her turquoise-blue bag, she shrugged her shoulders in absolute detachment. Beyond the Park, the white walls of Aunt Luella's house twinkled behind the screen of a drooping branch. Rachel's cheeks went up into charming curves; she was smiling at William.

'If you did,' she said, 'it wouldn't come off. Aunt Luella would blink and twiddle her beads and say "Listen to William; isn't he wonderful!" and Patsey and Everard would go on chastely squeezing each other's hands. I'm afraid you can't be direct. Besides, you really can't give them chapter and verse. Mother would be so upset. Besides, I don't want Everard made an idiot of. He's right according to his lights. The last thing I want is to score off the poor old thing. He did do me one good turn; he pulled me out of my hole, and, as I say, he did seem to be an experience. No, William, don't shoot him up. All we have to work for is the protection of Patsey. He must be quietly blighted. That's up to you, I feel. As the man of the family, you really do carry some weight with Aunt Luella. Simply be rather heavy. Tell her . . . tell her you've heard the most shocking things about Everard at Oxford. Say they're being said everywhere. If the worst comes to the worst, I'll support you, of course. But I think I should make the worst worse. You see, it's awkward for mother; she loathes Chummy instinctively; I think she must have some jungle instinct about him. But seeming to crab Patsey's marriage when she hasn't got me off—— And whenever she tries to say anything about Everard, Aunt Luella goes off like an alarm clock.'

'Oxford,' said William annoyed. 'Who in God's name would have heard of Chummy there? He's quite obscure, isn't he?'

'Oh, I suppose you all gossip,' said his cousin, indifferent. 'Like men always do.' She laid her gloved hand with the diamond bracelet over his for a moment. 'William,' she said, 'be effective. I count on you absolutely. Do go back and be effective at once, *now*. Then come round and let's go out to dinner and hear how effective you've been.'

Shaking out her blue dress with a gesture, his cousin was gone. The June sun seemed to William paler; a very slight shiver went down his back.

As William paced round the morning-room, waiting for Aunt Luella, he asked himself once more what this fuss was about. He tried to pull out an antique-looking book from a rack, to discover this opened, revealing a vanity-box. He brushed his nose nervously over some prim yellow roses which were scentless and which, unbalanced, flopped heavily from the vase. He seated himself abruptly in an armchair which, mounted on springs, sank under him. Unnerved, he stood up with his back to the empty grate, repeating that values were relative. He glared at the children racing around in the Park and thought what a pity it was that the race need go on.

His Aunt Luella sent urgent messages, wanting to know

why he wouldn't join them for tea. Perhaps she would never come. Suppose she sent Everard?

Then he heard her plunging along in that characteristic way, her necklace swinging against her belt-buckle. She shot in with the light on her spectacles, glittering at him reproachfully. 'William, you're *too* naughty! You mustn't be such a shy boy. Chummy is most disappointed. I never heard——'

'It's not that,' said her nephew. 'I never have been a shy boy. I've got heaps to say when I'm let get a word in edgeways. I've got heaps to say about Everard. Aunt Luella, this marriage——'

' — *Dear* Everard!' she exclaimed, and, as Rachel had said, went off like an alarm clock. Going on talking, she put out a hand for William's and made him sit down by her on the window-seat. 'Dear Chummy,' she finished, 'I do admire him so. Happiness makes him *solemn*.'

'He may have cause to be solemn. Do you really *know*, Aunt Luella, that he is in every way a suitable husband for Patsey?'

'Almost anyone would be — anyone *nice*. She'd make anyone into a good husband. That's her gift, I've always thought. It's sheer bad luck that it's never come into play. Dear Patsey . . .'

'I'm sorry,' said William, standing up with an effort. 'I'm afraid I've got to be a bit of a brute. It's up to me — I mean there seems no one else — I mean, as a man — I'm afraid Everard *isn't* nice. He won't do. Certain things have come to my knowledge—— We must face facts.'

'Don't talk,' said his aunt with asperity, 'about what you know nothing about.'

'I'm sorry,' repeated William, 'but I've been given to understand——'

'My dear boy, you're too young to understand anything.'

'I merely happen to know,' said her nephew, scarlet, 'that he made improper suggestions to a young girl.'

'*My-dear-boy*——' said his aunt. She looked from his chin to his shoes, blinked quickly behind her glasses, let out a small smothered hysterical sound like a whinny, then pressed her handkerchief violently to her lips. She was leaning back with her shoulder against the shutter: the shutter shook. William thrust his hands deep into his pockets and feelingly looked away from her.

The shutter still shook, and small noises exploded from his aunt's handkerchief. 'Aunt Luella,' said William, 'do pull yourself together. We've got to do something, haven't we?'

Aunt Luella meekly lowered her handkerchief from a mouth twisted in uncontrollable mirth. 'Dear William,' she faltered, 'I'm so awfully sorry. But you were so dramatic. Now, *who's* been giving our poor Rachel away?'

William froze by the table, opening the shagreen blotter. 'Oh, so you've found out?'

'I know,' his aunt said grimly, 'the real *facts* of the matter. Who's been telling you fairy-tales? . . . I suppose,' she darted out at him, 'Rachel has?'

William nodded cautiously. Aunt Luella stared into the air between them. 'Oh!' she exclaimed. 'The *unscrupulous* girl she is!'

William gulped. 'I laughed for a moment,' his aunt explained indignantly. 'William, of course you are *wax* in that girl's hands. All boys are. Of course you don't know Rachel! If there ever was "still water!" Just one mass of jealous subtlety. She cannot bear to see Patsey happy this way. We all know she stops at nothing. But even so ——'

'Didn't it rather shock you?'

'Shock me! My dear boy, at your age you cannot *imagine* what that poor Everard's been through. She's been his bad

angel. Of course, she made a dead set at him. If ever a girl
tried to wreck a man! And Chummy, being so conscientious
and good all the time, trying to live his miserable marriage
down. Told me? Of course he told me; he was so splendid
about it, trying to shield that little minx all the way through.
He was so distressed for us all when she walked in one day
and he found she was Patsey's cousin. *She* never turned a hair.
Of course he told me; Chummy and I are *friends*! He said he
did feel, as things were, that I ought to know. But Chummy
doesn't bear malice!'

'Anxious to get in first,' observed William gloomily.

His aunt, glaring, continued, ' "I only want," poor
Everard said, "to shield Patsey. We must think first of her."
That was of course what we both felt. And of course we kept
poor dear Héloïse out of it. Though I must say it's what she
deserves. Always saving Serbian children and looking
superior. I could have told her Rachel would come to no
good. But, really, her spite surprises me. And her effrontery.
My first instinct was, of course, never to have her here again.
But then dear Patsey'd have wondered. She asked him to take
her abroad *in his wife's car!*'

'Aunt Luella,' said William, 'you shock me. How can you
believe a swine who talks like that about Rachel! How can
you let a person like that marry your Patsey!'

'I know the girl only too well,' his aunt said with gloomy
triumph. 'For years I've seen this coming. I'm sorry for *you*,
William. I don't like to disillusion a boy of your age. I
wouldn't like you to feel you have made a fool of yourself.'

(Of this she gave small indication.) 'But there's only
Rachel to thank. No, I'm not angry. I'm merely sorry for
you.'

It struck William, whose relations with Aunt Luella had
up to now been affable, suave and pleasant, that they were

now in the thick of a raging row. She was rather certainly hating him. He felt like the dog in the Anstey story that inconveniently dug up the shot poodle. The familiar air of her beetle-green room reproached him. The cigarette-box recalled sharply arrears of her hospitality, their pleasant chats about documents. He gazed at his aunt, whose mauve colour rose steadily: he had never seen Aunt Luella change colour before. His heart dropped an inch.

'My God,' he thought, 'am I wrong?' He couldn't believe this was normal family life. 'Is this mother love?' he wondered, and pictured a large red hen. Or could there be something subtler, nearer the quick, as it were, the matter with Aunt Luella? 'Confound all women,' he thought. He said obstinately: '*I* think Rachel comes out of this well. I'm sorry her name was ever brought into this. She simply wanted to save you and Patsey from——'

'She didn't,' snapped Aunt Luella; 'she wanted to wreck the marriage.' Frantic with indignation, she tugged at her amber string; the string snapped and the beads clattered about the floor. This gave William the sense of a last catastrophe; he went hopelessly down on his knees to gather the beads up.

'Stop crawling about,' said his aunt, 'and listen to me, William. I could have never believed that even a boy of your age could be so clumsy and stupid. You act like a child of five. You make it difficult for me ever to have you or Rachel about in this house again. If it were not for your Aunt Héloïse, I should advise you not to see Rachel again. She's an extremely bad influence.'

'Here are six of your beads,' said William with dignity. 'You'd be sorry to lose them. As it happens, I'm dining with her tonight.'

'Will you *listen* to what I'm saying?'

'I'm sorry this ... outbreak ... should have occurred,

Aunt Luella. I'd no idea I'd upset you. But I can't regret having spoken. You seem to me on the verge of a fearful mistake. I feel bound, as the man of the family——'

'Man? My dear child, you've only just left school. Yes, I quite see you're sorry. But you really should learn you're too young to meddle with things. We won't say any more about it, only please try and remember another time that you don't know *every*thing yet. Now do go and flatten your hair down and wash your face and get cool. Then come and have tea and talk nicely to Patsey and Everard. Of course, we'll forget this. I'm sure you meant very well.' She approached and patted his shoulder.

William turned to the door. His aunt, now only too normal, looked after him quizzically. 'Yes, run along with you,' she said. 'And don't be so silly again. Stop; just come back and give your old auntie a kiss . . . There, *now* we're right again, aren't we? . . . Dear old William. How nice that we don't, as a family, ever have grievances.'

His aunt's kiss still damp on his cheek, he succeeded in leaving the room.

.   .   .   .

William rang up the Ivy to book a table for two. As he crossed the landing he heard, through the drawing-room door above a rich male voice talking affably. He heard a tinkle of glass and excited, delighted laughter from Aunt Luella and Patsey.

'Well, if I *must*——' said the voice with beautiful resignation.

'Yes, you *must*, Everard; mustn't Everard, mummy?'

'Of course he must. Come along, don't be silly, Chummy!'

'Well, if I *must* . . .' William heard a siphon go off.

'Mummy, where's that other table? It's higher.'

'No, wait, Chummy — let me!'

'Well, if you really *will* insist . . .' Someone moved a table up for Everard's drink. 'No, let me light it!' cried Patsey. Later, she dropped the match-box. The Man of the Family was very much in possession.

'It really doesn't much matter,' thought William. 'They're all fools.'

THE NEEDLECASE

T HE car was sent to the train — along the straight road between dykes in the late spring dusk — to bring back Miss Fox, who was coming to sew for a week. Frank, the second son of the house, had come suddenly back from town; he was pleased to find the car there, which was more than he hoped, but appalled to see Miss Fox, in black, like a jointed image, stepping in at the back. Frank had, and wished to have, no idea who she was. So he sat in front with the chauffeur, looking glumly left at the willows and dykes flitting by, while Miss Fox, from the back, looked as fixedly out at willows and dykes at the other side of the road. No one spoke. They turned in at the lodge gates and the avenue trees closed in.

When the car drew up at the hall door, Frank got out and shouted. It embarrassed him having come home, and he did not want to explain. His sister Angela, sitting up at her window, heard, shot downstairs and flung her arms round his neck, nearly knocking him over, like far too big a dog, as though he had been away two years instead of two days. This pleasure she over-expressed was perfectly genuine; Angela was effusive because she was often depressed; she could not be bothered being subtle with Frank, whom she knew far too well, and whose chagrins she often shared. So she kept up this rowdy pretence that everything was for the best.

'Had-a-good-time?' she said.

'No.'

'I'm sure you did really,' said Angela.

'No doubt you know best,' said Frank. 'Who in God's name's that in there?'

'Oh, that's Miss *Fox*,' explained Angela, peering into the car, where Miss Fox sat like an image, waiting to be let out. Angela rang the bell wildly for someone to come and cope. The chauffeur carried Frank's bag and the sewing-woman's strapped-up brown paper suitcase up the wide steps. The front of the house loomed over them, massive and dark and cold: it was the kind of house that easily looks shut up, and, when shut up, looks derelict. Angela took Frank's arm and they went indoors, into the billiard-room, the only place they could be certain of meeting nobody else. The room had a dank, baizey smell, and a smell of cold anthracite from the unlit stove: four battered green shades hung low over the sheeted table. It was not cheery in here. Frank sat on the fender-stool with his shoulders up and stared through his sister Angela heavily, uninvitingly. Had he wished to be quite alone he would not, however, have shouted.

'What did you do?' said Angela.

'Nothing special,' Frank said. He had been up to London to meet a man who might get him a job if he liked the looks of him, and the man clearly had not. The man had seen Frank to do Arthur a good turn: unfortunately the brothers did not resemble each other. Everyone liked Arthur. And Frank had stayed up in London, and had hoped to stay longer, because of a girl, but that had been a flop too: he had run through his money; that was why he was home. Angela had the good sense to ask no more. Leaning against the table and screwing her left-hand white coral ear-ring tighter (she always looked rather well) she said nonchalantly: 'The Applebys have been over. Hermione's after Arthur. They want us for tennis on Monday. The vet. came about Reno; he says it's nothing — oh, and mother has heard from Arthur; he's coming

down Friday week and bringing his new girl. So then mother
wired to hurry on Miss Fox. She's going to make us all over —
first the drawing-room covers, then mother's black lace, and
then do up Toddy and me — cut about some dresses and run
up some tennis frocks. She's our one hope for the summer.
No doubt she sews like hell, but we really couldn't look
worse. Could we, Frank? I mean, could we?'

'Yes,' said Frank. 'I mean, no.'

'We heard of her through Aunt Doris,' said Angela, chatting away. 'She's one of the wonderfully brave — she's got a
child to support that she shouldn't have. She trained somewhere or other, so I suppose she *can* make. She's been on
these rounds for years, going down in the world a bit. She
seems dirt cheap, so there must be something fishy. She used
to work, years ago, for the Fotheringhams, but Aunt Doris
only got on to her after she fell.

'You surprise me,' said Frank, yawning drearily, wanting a
drink more than anything in the world.

Miss Fox's arrival, though perfectly unassuming, had left
quite a wake of noise: she had been taken up and put somewhere, but doors went on opening and shutting, Frank's
mother stood out in the hall giving directions, and his elder
sister Toddy began shouting for Angela. As Frank crossed
the hall his mother broke off to give him her vivid mechanical
smile and say, 'Oh, you're *back*.' The house — far too big
but kept on for Arthur, who was almost always away but
liked to think of it there — had many high windows and a
white stone well staircase that went, under a skylight, up and
up and up. This would have been an excellent house for
someone else to have lived in, and heated; Frank and Angela
could then have visited comfortably there. As it was, it was
like a disheartened edition of Mansfield Park. The country
around it was far too empty and flat.

Miss Fox was not to work tonight; they left her to settle in. But Toddy was in such a hurry to get in first with her things that she slipped upstairs, unobtrusively, as soon as dinner was over. She found Miss Fox still smoking over her supper tray. She was of that difficult class that has to have trays all the time. Too grand for the servants, she had to be fed in her room — one of those top bedrooms in any Georgian house with high ceilings and windows down by the floor. It looked rather bleak in the light of two hanging bulbs. A massive cheval glass, brought from downstairs today, reflected Miss Fox's figure sitting upright at the table. Deal presses stood round the walls, dress-boxes tottered in stacks and two dressmaker's dummies — one stout and one slimmer — protruded their glazed black busts. A sewing-machine with a treadle awaited the dressmaker's onslaught. In the grate, a thin fire rather uncertainly flapped. What should be done had been done to acclimatize Miss Fox. But her purpose here could be never far from her mind, for she rigidly sat at the table where she would work. A folded-back magazine was propped on the coffee-pot: when Toddy came in she lifted her eyes from this slowly, but did not attempt to rise.

Her meek, strong, narrow, expressionless face, with heavy eyelids, high cheekbones and secretive mouth, framed in dusty fair hair brushed flat and knotted behind, looked carven under the bleak overhead light. Its immobile shadows were startling. Toddy thought: 'She's important.' But this was absurd.

Toddy kicked the door to behind her and stood stock still, a cascade of tired dance dresses flung over one arm, two bales of gingham for tennis frocks balanced under the other. Success this forthcoming summer was deadly important, for Toddy was now twenty-four. She felt Miss Fox held her fate in the palm of her hand. So she stood stock still and did not know how to begin. She had quieter manners, a subtler air than Angela, but was in fact a rather one-idea girl.

'I hope you have all you want,' she said helplessly.

'Yes, thank you, Miss Forrester.'

'I mustn't disturb you tonight. But I thought you might like some idea——'

'Show me,' said Miss Fox politely, and pushed her chair back from the table

'My red tulle is ripped right round It caught on a spur——'

She stopped, for Miss Fox was looking at her so oddly, as though she were a ghost, as though it were terror and pleasure to see her face. Toddy's looks were not startling, but were, like her brother Arthur's, pleasant enough. No one, no man, had been startled this way before.

'It caught on a spur,' she said, on a rising note.

Miss Fox's eyes went quite blank. 'Tch-tch-tch,' she said, and bent quickly over the stuff. She had unpacked and settled in — Toddy saw, looking round — screens hid her bed and washstand, the facts of her life, away, but one or two objects had appeared on the mantelpiece, and a fine, imposing work-basket stood at her elbow. Toddy, who loved work-baskets, had a touch of the jackdaw, so, while Miss Fox was examining the martyred red dress, she flicked back the hinged lid of the basket and with innocent, bird-like impertinence routed through its contents. All sorts of treasures were here; 'souvenir' tape-measures, tight velvet emery bags, button-bags, a pin-cushion inside a shell, scissors of all sorts in scabbards — and oh, such a needle-case! 'As large as a family Bible,' said Toddy, opening it, pleased. And, like a family Bible, it had a photo stuck inside. 'Oh, what a nice little boy!' — '*Thank you*,' exclaimed Miss Fox, and with irresistible quickness, a snatch, had the needlecase back. The movement so surprising, it seemed not to have happened.

'That looked such a dear little boy,' Toddy went on, impenitent.

'My little nephew,' Miss Fox said impenetrably.

It was odd to think she had a child, for with such a nun-like face she had looked all wrong, somehow, smoking a cigarette. The dusty look of her hair must be the effect of light, for Toddy, standing above her, looked down and saw how well brushed her hair was. Her fingers looked as though they would always be cold, and Toddy dreaded their touch on her naked spine when the time would come to try on her evening dresses. And felt frightened alone with her, at the top of this dark, echoing house. They saved light everywhere, you had to grope up the stairs, for this well of a house drank money. So its daughters, likely to wither, had few 'advantages'. Everyone knew, Arthur knew, that Arthur must marry money. Toddy was sick of the sacrifice. She was in love this year, baulked all the time, and her serene, squarish face concealed a constant, pricking anxiety.

'I've *got* to look nice,' she said suddenly.

'I'll do all I can,' said Miss Fox, flashing up once again that odd, reminiscent look.

'How *like* you, Toddy,' Angela cried at breakfast.

'What was like Toddy?' Frank asked, scrawling a maze among the crumbs by his plate. He seldom listened to what his sisters were saying, but sat on at table with them because he had nowhere special to go next.

'Creeping up there, then poking about in her things. You really might give the poor old creature a break.'

'She's not so old,' said Toddy, serene. 'And the child looked about seven.'

'What was it like?'

'I only saw curls and a collar—I tell you, she snatched it away.'

'What child?' said Frank. He pushed his cup across vaguely and Angela gave him more coffee, but it was cold.

'The child she had,' said Toddy.

'Oh God,' said Frank, 'is she fallen?' But he did not care in the least.

'I told you she was, last night,' said Angela, hurt.

That morning, Miss Fox was put in the drawing-room to work. Bales of chintz were unrolled and she cut out the new covers, shaping them over the backs of the chairs with pins. In cold, windy April sunlight she crawled round and round the floor, with pins in her mouth. The glazed chintz looked horribly cold. Frank, kept so short of money, not only thought the rosy-and-scrolly pattern itself obscene, but found these new covers a frenzied extravagance. But now Arthur's most promising girl was coming to stay, and must at all costs be impressed. If she did marry Arthur, she'd scrap these covers first thing. Any bride would. Frank leaned in the doorway, letting a draught in that rustled under the chintz, to watch Miss Fox at work on her thankless task. She magnetized his idleness. Their silence was fascinating, for if he spoke she would have to spit out those pins. The drawing-room was full of tables covered with photographs: Arthur at every age. He watched Miss Fox dodge the tables and drag her lengths of chintz clear.

Then she sat back on her heels. 'How fast you get on,' Frank said.

'I give my whole mind to it.'

'Don't your hands get cold, touching that stuff?'

'They may do; I'm not particular.'

She put pins back in her mouth and Frank wondered how she had ever been seduced. He picked up her big scissors idly and snipped at the air with them. 'This house is like ice,' he said. 'Do you know this part of the world?'

She was round at the back of the sofa and nothing came for some time; she must be eyeing the pattern and chewing the pins. Then her voice came over the top. 'I've heard speak of it. It seems very quiet round here.'

'*Quiet*——' began Frank.

But, hearing his voice, his mother looked in and said with her ready smile: 'Come, Frank, I want you a moment. We mustn't disturb Miss Fox.'

That same afternoon, the sun went in. Sharp dark clouds with steely white edges began bowling over the sky and their passing made the whole landscape anxious and taut. Frank went out riding with Angela; the wind, coming up and up, whistled among the willows; the dykes cut the country up with uneasy gleams. The grass was still fawn-coloured; only their own restlessness told them that it was spring. It *was* quiet round here. They jogged tamely along, and Angela said she saw no reason why things should ever happen, and yet they did. She wished they saw more of life. Even Miss Fox in the house was *something*, she said, something to talk about, something going on. 'And of course I do need those clothes. But when we *are* all dressed up, I don't know where we're to go. Oh hell, Frank. I mean, really.' She rode hatless, the wind stung her cheeks pink: Frank bitterly thought that she looked like some Academy picture about the Morning of Life.

'Do you think Arthur'll marry that girl?'

'I daresay he'll try,' said Frank.

'Oh, come. You know, Frank, our Arthur's a big success ... It's terrible how we wonder about Miss Fox. Do you think we are getting prurient minds? But the idea's fantastic.'

'Fantastic,' Frank agreed, feeling his own despondency ironed into him. Angela shot off and galloped across the field.

That night, in a wind direct from the Ural mountains, the house began to creak and strain like a ship. The family sat downstairs with as few lights on as possible. It was Angela who slipped up to talk to Miss Fox. The handsome workbasket was present but hasped shut, and Angela, honourably, turned her eyes from it. She really did want to talk. She sat on the rug by the grate; the wind puffed down the chimney occasional gusts of smoke that made her eyes smart. Miss Fox sat at the table, puffing away at a cigarette with precision. Perhaps she was glad of company. Nothing showed she was not. Her head, sculptured by shadows, was one of the finest heads that Angela had ever seen.

'You must see a lot of funny things, going from house to house.'

'Well yes, I do. I do see some funny things.'

'Of course, so do hospital nurses. But people must be much funnier trying on clothes. And some families are mares' nests. I wish you'd tell me . . .'

'Oh well, that would hardly do.'

'You know nurses aren't discreet . . . My brother Frank thinks you're a witch.'

'Gentlemen will have their fun,' said Miss Fox, with an odd inflection, as though she were quoting. Meeting Angela's eye, she smiled her held-in, rigid smile. Angela thought with impatience of gentlemen's fun that they must have — and, in this connection, of Arthur, who had his share. She heard the wind gnaw at the corners of this great tomb of a house that he wouldn't let them give up.

'It's all right for Arthur,' she said.

'Those photographs in the drawing-room — they are all your Mr. Arthur?'

'Of course,' said Angela crossly.

'Miss Toddy favours him, doesn't she?'

Angela hugged her knees and Miss Fox got no answer to this. So the sewing-woman reached out her cold hand across the table, shook out of the packet and lit with precision another thin cigeratte. Then: 'I've seen Mr. Arthur,' she said.

'Oh yes, I've seen Mr. Arthur. He was staying one time in a lady's house where I worked. There were several young gentlemen there, and I wasn't, of course, in the way of hearing their names. They were a big party, ever so gay and high-spirited, dodging all over the house, they used to be, every night, and in and out of my workroom, playing some game. I used to be sitting alone, like I sit here, and they used to stop for a word as they went through, or sometimes get me to hide them. Pleasant, they all were. But I never did catch any names. Mr. Arthur took a particular fancy to one of my dummies, and asked me to lend it him to dress up for some game. I should have known better; I ought to have known my place.

'But it was eight years ago. The last night, I let him take the dummy away. They did laugh, I heard. But there was an accident and Mr. Arthur let it drop on the stairs. The pedestal broke and some of the skirt-wires bent. He came back, later, to tell me how sorry he was. He *was* sorry, too. He said he'd make it all right. But he went off next day, and I suppose something happened to put it out of his head. My lady was not at all pleased, as she had had the dummy made to her own figure, and her figure was difficult. I didn't work there again.'

'How like him!' exclaimed his sister, savagely reclasping her hands round her knees.

Miss Fox, immensely collected, let out a cloud of smoke. 'He meant no harm,' she said stonily.

Frank came upstairs in the dark, feeling his way by the handrail and calling, 'Angela?' It gave him the creeps when anyone disappeared. And downstairs Toddy was fumbling on the piano. 'Here,' called Angela. Frank knocked once,

and came in. 'You look very snug,' he said, rather resentfully.
This room's being inhabited gave the house a new focus.
Soon they would all be up here. He came and stood by the
fire and watched his sister rocking and hugging her knees.
He saw by her face that he had cut in on a talk. His own
superfluity bit him.

'Miss Fox once knew Arthur, Frank.'

'A ladder's run right down your stocking,' said Frank with
angry irrelevance.

'Damn,' said Angela vaguely.

'Best catch it up,' said Miss Fox.

She looked from Frank to Angela. There was a pause.
Then, in the most businesslike way, she put down her cigarette, opened her work-basket, glanced at Angela's stocking and,
matching it with her eye, drew a strand from a mixed plait
of darning silks. Then she took out the big black needlecase.
'Mr. Frank . . .' she said. He went over and, taking the case,
brought it across to Angela. She knelt upon the hearthrug;
he rested a hand on her shoulder and felt the shoulder go stiff.
'What a lot of needles,' she said mechanically. She and Frank
both stared at the photograph of the child. They saw, as
Toddy had seen, its curls and its collar. Like Arthur's collar
and curls in old photographs downstairs. And between the
collar and curls, Arthur's face stared back again at the uncle
and aunt.

'I should take a number five needle,' said Miss Fox calmly.

'I have,' said Angela, closing the needlecase.

'Ladders down stockings break one's heart,' said Miss Fox.

THE APPLE-TREE

'FRIGHTENED?' exclaimed Lancelot. 'Of her? Oh, non-sense — surely? She's an absolute child.'

'But *that's* what I mean,' said Mrs. Bettersley, glancing queerly sideways at him over the collar of her fur coat. He still did not know what she meant, and did not think she knew either.

In a rather nerve-racking combination of wind and moon-light Simon Wing's week-end party picked its way back to his house, by twos and threes, up a cinder-path from the village. Simon, who entered with gusto into his new role of squire, had insisted that they should attend the Saturday con-cert in the village memorial hall, a raftered, charmless and icy building endowed by himself and only recently opened. Here, with numbing feet and spines creeping, they had occupied seven front seats, under a thin but constant spate of recitation, pianoforte duet and part-song, while upon them from all quarters draughts directed themselves like arrows. To restore circulation they had applauded vigorously, too often precipitating an encore. Simon, satisfied with his friends, with his evening, leant forward to beam down the row. He said this would please the village. Lancelot communicated to Mrs. Bettersley a dark suspicion: this was really why Simon had asked them down.

'So I'm afraid,' she replied. 'And for church tomorrow.'

All the same, it had warmed them all to see Simon happy. Mounting the platform to propose a vote of thanks to the

Vicar, the great ruddy man had positively expanded and
glowed; a till now too palpable cloud rolled away from him.
It was this recognition by his old friends of the old Simon — a
recognition so instantaneous, poignant and cheerful that it
was like a handshake, a first greeting — that now sent the
party so cheerfully home in its two and threes, their host
boisterously ahead. At the tail, lagging, Lancelot and Mrs.
Bettersley fell into a discussion of Simon (his marriage, his
ménage, his whole aspect) marked by entire unrestraint; as
though between these two also some shadow had dissipated.
They were old friendly enemies.

'But a child——' resumed Lancelot.

'Naturally I didn't mean to suggest that she was a
werewolf!'

'You think she *is* what's the matter?'

'Obviously there's nothing funny about the *house*.'

Obviously there was nothing funny about the house.
Under the eerie cold sky, pale but not bright with moonlight,
among bare windshaken trees, the house's bulk loomed,
honourably substantial. Lit-up windows sustained the party
with promise of indoor comfort: firelight on decanters,
room after room heavy-curtained, Simon's feeling for
home made concrete (at last, after wandering years) in
deep leather chairs, padded fenders, and sectional book-
shelves, 'domes of silence' on yielding carpets: an unaspiring,
comfortable sobriety.

'She does seem to me only half there,' confessed Lancelot.
'Not, of course, I mean mentally, but——'

'She had that frightful time — don't you know? *Don't* you
know?' Mrs. Bettersley brightened, approaching her lips to
his ear in the moonlight. 'She was at that school — don't you
remember? After all *that*, the school broke up, you know.
She was sent straight abroad — she'd have been twelve at the

178

time, I dare say; in a pretty state, I've no doubt, poor child! —
to an aunt and uncle at Cannes. Her only relations; they lived
out there in a villa, never came home — she stayed abroad
with them. It was there Simon met her; then — all this.'

'School?' said Lancelot, stuttering with excitement. 'What
— were they ill-treated?'

'Heavens, not that,' exclaimed Mrs. Bettersley; 'worse——'

But just at this point — it was unbearable — they saw the
party pull up and contract ahead. Simon was waiting to
shepherd them through the gate, then lock the gate after
them.

'I hope,' he said, beaming, as they came up, 'you weren't
too bored?'

They could not fail to respond.

'It's been a marvellous evening,' said Mrs. Bettersley;
Lancelot adding, 'What wonderful talent you've got round
here.'

'I don't think we're bad for a village,' said Simon modestly,
clicking the gate to. 'The Choral Society are as keen as
mustard. And I always think that young Dickinson ought to
go on the stage. I'd pay to see him anywhere.'

'Oh, so would I,' agreed Lancelot cordially. 'It's too sad,'
he added, 'your wife having missed all this.'

Simon's manner contracted. 'She went to the dress
rehearsal,' he said quickly.

'Doesn't she act herself?'

'I can't get her to try . . . Well, here we are; here we are!'
Simon shouted, stamping across the terrace.

Young Mrs. Wing had been excused the concert. She had
a slight chill, she feared. If she ever did cast any light on
village society, it was tonight withheld. No doubt Simon
was disappointed. His friends, filing after him through the
French window into the library, all hoped that by now — it

was half-past ten — young Mrs. Simon might have taken her chill to bed.

But from the hearth her flat little voice said: 'Hullo!' There she stood, looking towards the window, watching their entrance as she had watched their exit. Her long silver sheath of a dress made her almost grown up. So they all prepared with philosophy to be nice to young Mrs. Wing. They all felt this first week-end party, this incursion of old friends all so much knit up with each other, so much knit up round Simon, might well be trying for young Mrs. Wing. In the nature even, possibly, of an ordeal. She was barely nineteen, and could not, to meet them, be expected to put up anything of 'a manner'. She had them, however, at a slight disadvantage, for Simon's marriage had been a shock for his friends. He had been known for years as a likely marrying man; so much so that his celibacy appeared an accident; but his choice of a wife — this mannerless, sexless child, the dim something between a mouse and an Undine, this wraith not considerable as a mother of sons, this cold little shadow across a hearth — had considerably surprised them. By her very passivity she attacked them when they were least prepared.

Mrs. Wing, at a glance from her husband, raised a silver lid from some sandwiches with a gesture of invitation. Mrs. Bettersley, whose appetite was frankly wolfish, took two, and, slipping out inch by inch from her fur coat, lined up beside her little hostess in the firelight, solid and brilliant. The others divided armchairs in the circle of warmth.

'Did you have a nice concert?' said Mrs. Wing politely. No one could answer. 'It went off well on the whole,' said Simon gently, as though breaking sorrowful news to her.

Lancelot could not sleep. The very comfort of bed, the too exquisite sympathy with his body of springs and mattress, became oppressive. Wind had subsided; moonlight sketched a window upon his floor. The house was quiet, too quiet; with jealousy and nostalgia he pictured them all sleeping. Mrs. Wing's cheek would scarcely warm a pillow. In despair Lancelot switched the light on; the amiable furniture stared. He read one page of *Our Mutual Friend* with distaste and decided to look downstairs for a detective story. He slept in a corridor branching off from the head of the main staircase.

Downstairs, the hall was dark, rank with cooling cigar-smoke. A clock struck three; Lancelot violently started. A little moon came in through the skylight; the library door was closed; stepping quietly, Lancelot made his way to it. He opened the door, saw red embers, then knew in a second the library was not empty. All the same, in there in the dark they were not moving or speaking.

Embarrassment — had he surprised an intrigue? — and abrupt physical fear — were these burglars? — held Lancelot bound on the threshold. Certainly someone in here was not alone; in here, in spite of the dark, someone was watching someone. He did not know whether to speak. He felt committed by opening the door, and, standing against the grey of the glass-roofed hall, must be certainly visible.

Finally it was Simon's voice that said defensively: 'Hullo?' Lancelot knew he must go away immediately. He had only one wish — to conceal his identity. But Simon apparently did not trust one; moving bulkily he came down the long room to the door, bumping, as though in a quite unfamiliar room, against the furniture, one arm stuck out ahead, as though pushing something aside or trying to part a curtain. He seemed to have no sense of space; Lancelot ducked, but a great hand touched his face. The hand was ice-cold.

'Oh, *you?*' said Simon. From his voice, his breath, he had

been drinking heavily. He must still be holding a glass in his other hand — Lancelot heard whisky slopping about as the glass shook.

'It's all right,' said Lancelot; 'I was just going up. Sorry,' he added.

'You can't — come — in —here,' said Simon obstinately.

'No, I say: I was just going up.' Lancelot stopped; friendliness fought in him with an intense repulsion. Not that he minded — though this itself was odd: Simon hardly ever touched anything.

But the room was a trap, a *cul-de-sac*; Simon, his face less than a yard away, seemed to be speaking to him through bars. He was frightful in fear; a man with the humility of a beast; he gave off fear like some disagreeable animal smell, making Lancelot dislike and revolt at his own manhood, subject to such decay.

'Go away,' said Simon, pushing at him in the dark. Lancelot stepped back in alarm; a rug slipped under his foot; he staggered grasping at the jamb of the door. His elbow knocked a switch; immediately the hall, with its four powerful lamps, sprang into illumination. One was staggered by this explosion of light; Lancelot put his hands over his eyes; when he took them away he could see Simon's face was clammy, mottled; here and there a bead of sweat trembled and ran down. He was standing sideways, his shoulder against the door; past him a path of light ran into the library.

Mrs. Simon stood just out of the light, looking fixedly up and pointing at something above her head. Round her Lancelot distinguished the big chairs, the table with the decanters, and faintly, the glazed bookcases. Her eyes, looking up, reflected the light but did not flicker; she did not stir. With an exclamation, a violent movement, Simon shut the library door. They both stood outside its white glossy panels. By

contrast with what stood inside, staring there in the dark
Simon was once more human; unconsciously as much to gain
as to impart reassurance, Lancelot put a hand on his arm.

Not looking at one another, they said nothing.

They were in no sense alone even here, for the slam of the
door produced in a moment or two Mrs. Bettersley, who
looked down at them from the gallery over the zone of
bright lights, her face sharpened and wolfish with vehement
curiosity. Lancelot looked up; their eyes met.

'All right; only somebody sleep-walking,' he called up softly.

'All right,' she replied, withdrawing; but not, he guessed,
to her room; rather to lean back in shadow against the wall of
the gallery, impassive, watchful, arms folded over the breast
of her dark silk kimono.

A moment later she still made no sign — he would have
been glad of her presence, For the return to Simon of sensibility and intelligence, like circulation beginning again in a limb
that had been tightly bound up, was too much for Simon.
One side-glance that almost contained his horror, then —
huge figure crumpling, swaying, sagging — he fainted suddenly. Lancelot broke his fall a little and propped him, sitting,
against the wall.

This left Lancelot much alone. He noted details: a dog-
collar lying unstrapped, ash trodden into a rug, a girl's gloves
— probably Mrs. Simon's — dropped crumpled into a big
brass tray. Now drawn to the door — aware the whole time
of his position's absurdity — he knelt, one ear to the keyhole.
Silence. In there she must still stand in contemplation —
horrified, horrifying — of something high up that from the not
quite fixity of her gaze had seemed unfixed, pendent, perhaps
swaying a little. Silence. Then — he pressed closer — a thud-
thud-thud — three times, like apples falling.

This idea of apples entered his mind and remained, frightfully clear; an innocent pastoral image seen black through a dark transparency. This idea of fruit detaching itself and, from a leafy height, falling in the stale, shut-up room, had the sharpness of hallucination: he thought he was going mad.

'Come down,' he called up to the gallery.

Mrs. Bettersley, with that expectant half-smile, appeared, looked over immediately, then came downstairs. Noting Simon's unconsciousness, for which she seemed to be grateful, she went to the library door. After a moment facing the panels she tried the handle, cautiously turning it.

'*She's* in there,' said Lancelot.

'Coming?' she asked.

He replied, 'No,' frankly and simply.

'Oh, well,' she shrugged; 'I'm a woman,' and entered the library, pushing the door to behind her. He heard her moving among the furniture. 'Now come,' she said. 'Come, my dear . . .' After a moment or two of complete silence and stillness: 'Oh, my God, no — I can't!' she exclaimed. She came out again, very white. She was rubbing her hands together as though she had hurt them. 'It's impossible,' she repeated. 'One can't get past . . . it's like an apple-tree.'

She knelt by Simon and began fumbling with his collar. Her hands shook. Lancelot watched the access of womanly busyness.

The door opened again and young Mrs. Wing came out in her nightgown, hair hanging over her shoulders in two plaits, blinking under the strong light. Seeing them all, she paused in natural confusion.

'I walk in my sleep,' she murmured, blushed, and slipped past upstairs without a glance at her husband, still in confusion, like any young woman encountered by strangers in her nightgown; her appearance and disappearance the very picture of modest precipitancy.

Simon began to come to. Mrs. Bettersley also retreated. The fewest possible people ought, they felt, to be in on this.

Sunday morning was milky-blue, mild and sunny. Mrs. Bettersley appeared punctually for breakfast, beaming, pink, and impassible. Lancelot looked pale and puffy; Mrs. Simon did not appear. Simon came in like a tempered Boreas to greet the party, rubbing his hands. After breakfast they stepped out through the window to smoke on the terrace. Church, said Simon pressingly, would be at eleven.

Mrs. Bettersley revolted. She said she liked to write letters on Sunday morning. The rest, with a glance of regret at the shining November garden, went off like lambs. When they had gone, she slipped upstairs and tapped on Mrs. Simon's door.

The young woman was lying comfortably enough, with a fire burning, a mild novel open face down on the counterpane. This pretty bride's room, pink and white, frilled and rosy, now full of church bells and winter sunshine, had for Mrs. Bettersley, in all its appointments, an air of anxious imitation and of approximation to some idea of the grown-up. Simon's bed was made and the room in order.

'You don't mind?' said Mrs. Bettersley, having sat down firmly.

Mrs. Simon said, nervously, she was so pleased.

'All right this morning?'

'Just a little chill, I think.'

'And no wonder! Do you often walk in your sleep?'

Mrs. Simon's small face tightened, hardened, went a shade whiter among the pillows. 'I don't know,' she said. Her manner became a positive invitation to Mrs. Bettersley to go away. Flattening among the bedclothes, she tried hard to obliterate herself.

Her visitor, who had not much time — for the bells had stopped; they would be back again in an hour — was quite merciless. 'How old were you,' she said, 'when *that* happened?'

'Twelve — please don't——'

'You never told anyone?'

'No — please, Mrs. Bettersley — please not now. I feel so ill.'

'You're making Simon ill.'

'Do you think I don't know!' the child exclaimed. 'I thought he'd save me. I didn't think he'd ever be frightened. I didn't know any power could ... Indeed, indeed, Mrs. Bettersley, I had no idea ... I felt so safe with him. I thought this would go away. Now when it comes it is twice as horrible. Do you think it is killing him?'

'I shouldn't wonder,' said Mrs. Bettersley.

'Oh, oh,' moaned Mrs. Wing, and, with wrists crossed over her face, shook all over, sobbing so that the bed-head rattled against the wall. 'He was so sorry for me,' she moaned; 'it was more than I could resist. He was so sorry for me. Wouldn't *you* feel Simon might save you?'

Mrs. Bettersley, moving to the edge of the bed, caught the girl's wrists and firmly but not untenderly forced them apart, disclosing the small convulsed face and staring eyes. 'We've got three-quarters of an hour alone,' she said. 'You've got to tell me. Make it come into words. When it's once out it won't hurt any more — like a tooth, you know. Talk about it like anything. Talk to Simon. You never have, have you? You never do?'

Mrs. Bettersley felt quite a brute, she told Lancelot later. She had, naturally, in taking this hard line, something to go on. Seven years ago, newspapers had been full of the Crampton Park School tragedy: a little girl's suicide. There had been some remarkable headlines, some details, profuse speculation. Influence from some direction having been brought to bear, the affair disappeared from the papers abruptly. Some suggestion of things having been 'hushed up' gave the affair, in talk, a fresh cruel prominence; it became a topic. One hinted at all sorts of scandal. The school broke up; the staff disappeared, discredited; the fine house and grounds, in the West Country, were sold at a loss. One pupil, Myra Conway, felt the shock with surprising keenness. She nearly died of brain fever; collapsing the day after the suicide, she remained at death's door for weeks, alone with her nurses in the horrified house, Crampton Park. All the other children were hurried away. One heard afterwards that her health, her nerves, had been ruined. The other children, presumably, rallied; one heard no more of them. Myra Conway became Myra Wing. So much they all knew, even Simon.

Myra Wing now lay on her side in bed, in her pink bedroom, eyes shut, cheek pressed to the pillow as though she were sleeping, but with her body rigid; gripping with both hands Mrs. Bettersley's arm. She spoke slowly, choosing her words with diffidence as though hampered by trying to speak an unfamiliar language.

'I went there when I was ten. I don't think it can ever have been a very good school. They called it a home school, I suppose because most of us stayed for the holidays — we had no parents — and none of us was over fourteen. From being there so much, we began to feel that this was the world. There was a very high wall round the garden. I don't think they were unkind to us, but everything seemed to go wrong. Doria and I were always in trouble. I suppose that was why we knew each other. There were about eighteen other girls, but none of them liked us. We used to feel we had some disease — so much so, that we were sometimes ashamed to meet each other: sometimes we did not like to be together. I don't think we knew we were unhappy; we never spoke of that; we should have felt ashamed. We used to pretend we were all right; we got in a way to be quite proud of ourselves, of being different. I think, though, we made each other worse. In those days I was very ugly. Doria was as bad; she was very queer-looking; her eyes goggled and she wore big round glasses. I suppose if we had had parents it would have been different. As it was, it was impossible to believe anyone could ever care for either of us. We did not even care for each other; we were just like two patients in hospital, shut away from the others together because of having some frightful disease. But I suppose we depended on one another.

'The other children were mostly younger. The house was very large and dark-looking, but full of pictures to make it look homely. The grounds were very large, full of trees and laurels. When I was twelve, I felt if this was the world I could not bear it. When I was twelve I got measles: another girl of my age got the measles, too, and we were sent to a cottage to get well. She was very pretty and clever; we made friends; she told me she did not mind me but she could not bear Doria. When we both got well and went back to the others, I loved her so much I felt I could not bear to part from her. She had a home of her own; she was very happy and gay; to know her and hear about her life was like heaven. I took great trouble to please her; we went on being friends. The others began to like me; I ran away from Doria. Doria was left alone. She seemed to be all that was horrible in my life; from the moment we parted things began to go right with me. I laughed at her with the others.

'The only happy part of Doria's life and mine in the bad days had been the games we played and the stories we told in a lonely part of the garden, a slope of lawn with one beautiful old apple-tree. Sometimes we used to climb up in the branches. Nobody else ever came there; it was like something of our own; to be there made us feel happy and dignified.

'Doria was miserable when I left her. She never wept; she used to walk about by herself. It was as though everything I had got free of had fallen on her, too: she was left with my wretchedness. When I was with the others I used to see her, always alone, watching me. One afternoon she made me come with her to the apple-tree; I was sorry for her and went; when we got there I could not bear it. I was so frightened of being lost again; I said terrible things to her. I wished she was dead. You see, there seemed to be no other world outside the school.

'She and I still slept in the same room, with two others. That night — there was some moon — I saw her get up. She tied the cord of her dressing-gown — it was very thick — round her waist tightly; she looked once at me, but I pretended to be asleep. She went out and did not come back. I lay — there was only a little moon — with a terrible feeling, like something tight round my throat. At last I went down to look for her. A glass door to the garden was open. I went out to look for her. She had hanged herself, you know, in the apple-tree. When I first got there I saw nothing. I looked round and called her, and shook the branches, but only — it was September — two or three apples fell down. The leaves kept brushing against my face. Then I saw her. Her feet were just over my head. I parted the branches to look — there was just enough moon — the leaves brushed my face. I crept back into bed and waited. No one knew; no steps came. Next morning, of course, they did not tell us anything. They said she was ill. I pretended to know no better. I could not think of anything but the apple-tree.

'While I was ill — I was very ill — I thought the leaves would choke me. Whenever I moved in bed an apple fell down. All the other girls were taken away. When I got well, I found the house was empty. The first day I could, I crept out alone to look for the real apple-tree. "It is only a tree," I thought; "if I could see it, I should be quite well." But the tree had been cut down. The place where it grew was filled with new turf. The nurse swore to me there had never been an apple-tree there at all. She did not know — no one ever knew — I had been out that night and seen Doria.

'I expect you can guess the rest — you were there last night. You see, I am haunted. It does not matter where I am, or who I am with. Though I am married now, it is just the same. Every now and then — I don't know yet when or what brings it about — I wake to see Doria get up and tie the cord round her waist and go out. I have to go after her; there is always the apple-tree. Its roots are in me. It takes all my strength, and now it's beginning to take Simon's.

'Those nights, no one can bear to be with me. Everyone who has been with me knows, but no one will speak of it. Only Simon tries to be there those times — you saw, last night. It is impossible to be with me; I make rooms impossible. I am not like a house that can be burnt, you see, or pulled down. You know how it is — I heard you in there last night, trying to come to me——'

'I won't fail again: I've never been more ashamed,' said Mrs. Bettersley.

'If I stay up here the tree grows in the room; I feel it will choke Simon. If I go out, I find it darker than all the others against the sky . . . This morning I have been trying to make up my mind; I must go; I must leave Simon. I see quite well this is destroying him. Seeing him with you all makes me see how he used to be, how he might have been. You see, it's hard to go. He's my life. Between all this . . . we're so happy. But make me do this, Mrs. Bettersley!'

'I'll make you do one thing. Come away with me — perhaps for only a month. My dear, if I can't do this, after last night, *I'm* ruined,' exclaimed Mrs. Bettersley.

The passion of vanity has its own depths in the spirit, and is powerfully militant. Mrs. Bettersley, determined to vindicate herself, disappeared for some weeks with the haunted girl. Lancelot, meanwhile, kept Simon company. From the ordeal their friend emerged about Christmas, possibly a little harder and brighter. If she had fought, there was not a hair displaced. She did not mention, even to Lancelot, by what arts, night and day, by what cynical vigilance, she had succeeded in exorcising the apple-tree. The victory aged her, but left her as disengaged as usual. Mrs. Wing was returned to her husband. As one would expect, from then on less and less was seen of the couple. They disappeared into happiness: a sublime nonentity.